THE FRANK DIARY OF ANNE
- AGED 14

D.J. Donaldson

Published in 2008 by YouWriteOn.com

Copyright © Text D.J. Donaldson

First Edition

Published by YouWriteOn.com

With thanks to my husband, Paul
for his patience, and for keeping me supplied with
endless cups of tea while I wrote this novel.

CONTENTS

CHAPTER ONE

Hove (Actually)

Wednesday 15 August

I can't believe I'm saying this - but I'm starting to look forward to going back to school. The summer holiday is really starting to drag. I think I'm even starting to get on OB's nerves. (OB is the nickname I give to my mum, Veronica Barrowman – it stands for Old Bag but don't tell her that!)

07:00

I've no idea why it's necessary for me to have to set the alarm so early when I'm supposed to be on holiday but I always get the same response from OB when I ask her.

"You can't stay in bed all day, young lady…you'll waste your life away!"

That answer is somewhere up there with the classic, "because I said so!"

I stare at the god-like images plastered all over my bedroom walls (all my favourite singers) for a while before throwing off my duvet, complete with its red Betty Boop cover, and dragging myself out of bed and throwing open the matching curtains to peer out of the window.

Oh my God! Our street's been invaded by coffin dodgers!

Although there's nothing actually wrong with old people, I have to admit to feeling more than slightly disturbed by the distinct lack of any sign of youth in this area of Brighton (well, Hove actually) – God, even I'm starting to sound like them now!

Why is it that, even though the two towns merged into each other years ago, the residents of Hove still seem to feel the need to separate themselves from their neighbours? I guess the older generation like to distance themselves from the bohemian image of Brighton. It's far too trendy and exciting for them.

The wrinklies do have their plus side though. They are funny and, if you can be bothered to talk to them, they have some interesting stories to tell - and they will always say hello in the street (something that would be way too un-cool to happen in Brighton).

07:05

"For goodness sake, Anne! How many times do I have to tell you not to scrape the chair across the floor?"

OB looks at me disapprovingly over the top of her trendy black-rimmed glasses. She pushes a stray lock of blonde hair off her face and tucks it behind her ear as she plonks a plate of freshly-made waffles on the kitchen table in front of me. Ignoring her nagging, I pick up my phone to send a text to my best friend, Stephanie. Maybe she wants to do something today?

WOT R U DOIN 2DAY?

"Anne, please put that thing down while you are at the table!" OB sighs.

A bleep from my mobile announces that Stephanie has replied so I read the screen.

DO U WNT 2 CM RND L8R?

Great! At least I can get out of here for the day. I'm so bored! I type my reply.

OK. CU AT 10.

Another bleep from my phone and the arrangements are confirmed.

XLNT. BCNU.

OB snatches the phone out of my hand and reads the text language. She lets out a disapproving sigh, and makes some sarcastic remark about proper spelling – or similar, I wasn't really listening. She places it on the table and gives me that, "You're grounded for a week if you so much as touch this phone before breakfast is over," look. I give her my, "I'm not bothered because I've finished with it anyway so don't think me not touching it has got anything to do with you!" look - and pour maple syrup on the now not so freshly-made waffles on my plate.

21:00

I seem to have the most naggy mum in the world. My friends' mums never seem to go on them all the time when I'm round their houses so I don't get why OB seems to feel the need to nag at me about every little thing I do. Thankfully, I manage to avoid her for the rest of the day. I take refuge in my bedroom, surrounded by my love gods and watch three Johnny Depp films on DVD, suddenly all is well with the world. (sigh!).

Thursday 16 August

OB and Anne do "What not to Wear". Remind me never to go shopping with her again – EVER!

08:30

"Come on Anne, I want to get to the shops *before* they close!"

Oh Great! A day's shopping with my mother. This is not something that I'm finding very appealing. Mind you, it's more appealing than the reason that we are going in the first place. She got it into her head that it would be a good idea for us to spend the last two weeks of my summer holidays on a cruise together. Two whole weeks stuck on a boat with her! I grit my teeth as I walk downstairs to embark on the mission to buy some "suitable" clothes for me to wear.

09:15

"Mum, I'm fourteen, not four!"

"Nonsense, it looks lovely. The flowers just make it look Summery."

I hang my head in shame as OB pays the smirking shop assistant and the hideous floral creation is placed in a large bag. It might have its place on a four year old bridesmaid, but for an evening dress on a Mediterranean cruise? This is going to be worse than I imagined!

09:45

"No way am I wearing this!"

"It'll be lovely and cool when we go out on excursions during the day...Oooh, look, Anne! They do it in three colours!"

Three dresses that looked as if they belonged on a tennis court were placed firmly over her arm. Pastel pink, yellow and blue – YUK! She'll be expecting me to wear short socks and sandals with it next!

09:46

Oh no, don't even think about it...Too late! She's picked up three matching pairs of ankle socks and a pair of white sandals. I'm definitely not letting her take any photos of me while we're away!

10:35

At last! We're getting somewhere. Three pairs of shorts and a selection of T-shirts from New Look – and a great pair of jeans. Things are looking up!

12:15

Time to stop for lunch (and to cool down before we kill each other!) Only swimwear, casual evening wear and shoes to go! We walk into Costa coffee bar and OB hands the bags of shopping to me. I find a table while she orders lunch.

"What's this?"

"A bacon and brie panini."

"But I wanted a cheese and ham toastie!"

"You need to develop your palate if you are going to enjoy the exotic food on the cruise!"

14

This has really confused me. She wants me to have a sophisticated palate and yet she wants to dress me up like a baby doll – WEIRD!

14:00

Still shopping – I'm getting really bored now!

17:30

Home at last!

Friday 17 August

Escaped for my last day of freedom before being locked up with OB for two weeks!

10:00

I open the door to Stephanie, my BFFL (Best Friend for Life!). We've been friends forever (well since we were three). We don't go to the same school any more. She goes to the local secondary school and I go to a private school so we don't see much of each other in the week – but we still see each other at weekends and school holidays.

I love Steph – She's the only person I know that it is Okay to be un-cool with. She doesn't care about wearing the latest fashion or having her hair in a "Posh" bob. She's completely chilled-out and spends most of her time in jeans, T-Shirt and trainers, with her light brown hair shoved back into a pony-tail. Today is no different. Sometimes I wish I could be more like her.

10:15

Me and Steph walk to The Meeting Place, a café on the seafront. We order milkshakes and take them over to a table by the windbreaks to drink. This is the best place to come and people watch in the Summer. The open air café is always full of people. I love coming here.

10:16

I've just remembered that it probably wasn't a good idea to come to this café after all. Being popular, there's always someone you know here – and, although I love her to bits, being seen with Steph is not exactly good for the image!

10:20

I'm totally mortified – a seagull just dumped its load on my head! Neither of us ever carry tissues so, without thinking, Steph rubs my head with the sleeve of her favourite jacket, transferring the mess from my hair onto her coat.

10:21

Having a major guilt trip about mentally dissing Steph earlier!

11:00

Fully recovered from the seagull trauma, we leave the café and walk along the seafront to the King Alfred Amusement Park.

11:05

We pass a fresh fish stall – you know the ones where the men selling fish can tell you exactly where they were caught and then gut them in front of you – Gross! Worse than that, the area is surrounded with seagulls.

"Look at that one on the roof of the stall, Anne. It's looking right at you. I bet it's the one that got you earlier!" cries Steph.

I peer up at the roof and spot the smug-looking bird. It does seem to be looking at me. Steph starts to howl with laughter and then runs around me doing a very loud impression of a seagull. She's sooooo embarrassing!

11:06

Earlier guilt trip is definitely easing!

11:30

We finally get to the King Alfred. There's a huge plastic tube that winds around the outside of the building. It's a sort of watery helter-skelter. We can see the swimmers ride down it before it re-enters the building and they splash into the swimming-pool inside. We sit on a bench and watch them for a while, eating a burger from the kiosk.

16:30

Arrived back home to finish packing. I've had a great time today though (apart from the Seagull bit!). Will miss Steph when I'm away.

Saturday 18 August

My two weeks of torture starts today! OB is really excited and says we should use this trip as a bonding exercise (Yeah, right!)

09:15

"I'd better just check that I've packed the passports and tickets!"

"Mum, will you please calm down! They'll be in exactly the same place as they were the last ten times you checked!

"I'm sorry darling. I'm getting over excited aren't I? It's just that I've never been on a girlie holiday before. We're going to have such a super time!"

OMG. She's acting like we're going on holiday as bessie mates! Someone pass me the sick bag please!

10.30

The poor taxi driver looked bored to death as he dropped us off at Gatwick Airport. OB talked him through the entire itinerary of the holiday in minute detail. What's she going to be like on the way back?

18:30

We've arrived in Rhodes! The flight wasn't too bad as OB read a book for most of the journey – at least it kept her quiet!

"Right! We've got all the bags. Now let me just check what we were supposed to do next," OB starts to rummage through her handbag.

"Mum…"

"Be quiet dear, I'm trying to find the piece of paper from the travel agent.   Ah, yes - Here it is!"

"But, Mum…"

"Will you be quiet for a minute – I'm trying to read!"

"Mum, there's a man over there with a board saying Sunshine Cruises."

OB reads out loud "You will be met by one of our representatives, who will take you to the ship. For your convenience, our representative will make themselves known by holding a board showing our company logo."

OB puts the paper back into her handbag and surveys the busy airport.

"Look, Anne, there's a man over there with a board saying Sunshine Cruises!"

This is going to be a *very* long two weeks!

18:40

There must be some mistake! Judging by the number of wrinklies on the coach, OB's booked us on a SAGA cruise! If that bloody Jane MacDonald's on that ship, I'm jumping overboard!

22:00

OB insists on unpacking the suitcases straight away.

"Well we don't want everything getting creased Anne," she says as she unpacks the cases, carefully removing the tissue paper from each garment.

Sunday 19 August

Day at sea. Will need this to find our sea legs!

07:30

Woken by loud "Bing-Bong!" coming from a speaker by my ear. Nearly jump out of my skin.

"Ladies and gentlemen,"

"What's going on? Who's talking to me!"

"We will start to serve breakfast in the main restaurant in approximately five minutes. At 09:00 Brian, our fitness trainer, will be holding an aerobics session by the swimming pool. In the cinema at 14:00, our film for today is Sleepless in Seattle. The captain will be holding a welcome cocktail party in the lounge at 21:30. May we take this opportunity of welcoming you all on board and wishing you a happy cruise – Bing-Bong!."

"Hi-de-Hi!" OB giggles.

"What?"

"It reminds me of that comedy programme – you know, the one set in a holiday camp. I can't remember what it was called though!"

08:30

After we've eaten a ginormous breakfast, OB insists on taking a stroll around the ship. I mooch beside her in my new shorts and t-shirt. She's attempting to do her best impression of a WAG as she struts around in her floaty dress, sun-glasses and huge floppy sunhat.

09:30

We manage to find our way out onto the main deck and stand to watch the aerobics class for a while. I have to admit that Brian, the instructor is pretty hot!

10:00

OB and me wander up to the front of the ship. I feel very pleased with myself as I do a witty impression of "Titanic".

OB puts her bag on the floor and pulls out a couple of towels to sunbathe on. She then proceeds to strip down to her bikini – which, to my horror, is microscopic!

"Come and sit down Anne. You need to learn to relax!"

"You need to learn to cover yourself up," I mutter under my breath as I notice the blokes driving the ship are visibly drooling at her while they watch her applying her sun-cream.

"I know just how Kate O'Mara felt now!" giggles OB

"Who?"

"Oh never mind!" she gets a book out of her bag and lays down to read.

10:05

I am completely devastated when three other people approach the front of the ship and all attempt to do an impression of "Titanic". Still, they weren't as good as mine!

21:30

I follow OB into the lounge in one of the "pretty" dresses OB picked out for me on our shopping trip. OB looks surprisingly glamorous in her black cocktail dress. I feel like a dork! To my horror, the cocktail party consists of a bloke playing some boring rubbish on the piano and everyone standing around talking.

22:00

Bored! I'm off to bed!

Monday 20 August

OB does Shirley Valentine – whoever that is?

07:30

Bing-Bong! "Ladies and gentlemen, breakfast is now available in the main restaurant. We will embark in Mykanos at 09:00. Please make sure that you are back at the meeting point by 12:30 to return to the ship. We hope you enjoy your excursion to the lovely island of Mykanos – Bing-Bong!."

"Hi-de-Hi!" OB giggles again.

Hilarious, mum! I reeeeally hope she's not going to do this every time they make an announcement.

08:45

We are ready to embark. OB has insisted that I wear one of the stupid tennis dresses that she bought for me. I look like I'm auditioning for the musical Annie – except my hair's sort of blonde!

10:30

Mykanos is really sweet. The harbour is surrounded by lots of white houses and amazing blue sea. You could almost imagine it as a film set!

It's hot here today – I'm beginning to think that OB was right about the tennis dress. I'm definitely not telling her that it's keeping me cool though.

11:30

We make our way back to the taverna where everyone is supposed to meet the tender, which will take us back to the ship.

OB orders us coffee and sits staring wistfully out at the sea. It does look beautiful, I have to admit. The midday sun is sparkling on the water, which looks exactly like the pictures you see in the travel brochures. Apparently they used this taverna in some film called Shirley Valentine in the 1980s. Nothing seems to happen in this island so it must have been a pretty boring film!

11:45

This place is weird! It seems to be full of middle-aged women – and they all seem to be asking the waiter his opinion on stretch marks. What's that about?

14:30

Brian saunters past OB and me as we are lazing on the sun-loungers by the pool. He is soooo buff! - Ugh! OB just gave him a really coy smile. Unbelievable! She's actually flirting with him. I mean, as if he'd be interested in an old bag like her!

21:00

There's a band playing in the lounge tonight. They're not too bad really. They've got most of the wrinklies up dancing anyway. I wish there was someone my own age to talk to!

21:10

Brian's just walked in. He looks just like a male model in his jeans and tight black shirt. OMG he's coming over! And he's smiling!

"Hi!" he smiles

"Hi!" OB and I both sigh.

"Fancy a dance?"

"That would be lovely," smiles OB as she slithers off her chair and floats onto the dance floor with him.

Noooooo! He can't possibly fancy her – she's my MUM!

Wednesday 22 August

Spent the day looking at a load of <u>really</u> old things. Some of them were even older than OB!!!

06:15

"Bing-Bong! Blah blah...Breakfast...blah blah...enjoy your excursion to Egypt – Bing-Bong!"

Wait for it...Hah! So Mrs Bing-Bong's even started to get on OB's nerves!

07:00

I try not to fall asleep as we wait in line to have our passports checked before we can enter Egypt.

07:30

Wish I could get back on the ship as the stench of Port Said fills my nostrils and the street-sellers, who are lining the gangplank, try to grab at us as we walk past. OB grasps my hand and hauls me towards the waiting coach.

07:31

Made it! Sit and wait while the rest of the traumatised passengers get on the coach and take their seats.

09:30

It's been two hours since we left Port Said, and I've yet to see anything other than sand! I've come to the conclusion that the pyramids must be the only thing in Egypt.

10:30

I'm shocked as I see beggars living in wooden shacks along the roadside of Cairo, right in front of huge buildings covered in gold. I think that the rich people should get rid of the gold and cover their houses in silver instead. That way, they would still have shiny houses but could give the extra money to the poor so they could buy a proper house. – I'm possibly a political genius! Maybe I should become a politician when I leave school.

10:45

The coach arrives in Giza. The guide explains that we would normally stop here to see the Sphinx. Unfortunately, it's covered in scaffolding so we drive past.

11:00

We finally reach the pyramids. The heat literally takes my breath away as we clamber off the coach. OB and I scramble back onto the coach and re-emerge armed with liquid.

11:02

"Is that it? - We've driven all that way for three triangles in the sand!"

"They're not triangles, Anne – they're pyramids!"

"Whatever!"

12:00

Lunch at the Cairo Hilton. We are told to help ourselves to a huge buffet that has been laid out for us. I haven't got a clue what most of it is and spend the whole of the meal trying to work out if the meat is camel or goat!

14:00

We then visit the Egyptian Museum to see Tutankhamun's treasures. It feels like an oven as we walk around the museum. It's impressive though, I've never seen so many jewels! Egypt must be a very rich country.

19:00

I'm too exhausted to care as the street-sellers try to stop us from getting back onto the ship. Have they been waiting here all day for us to get back or are these different ones?

20:00

I can't be bothered to join OB as she goes down to the lounge for a drink. I think the sun must have got to me because I fall asleep almost as soon as my head touches the pillow.

Friday 24 August

At last! A day off from visiting old relics!

08:00

Woken by OB's travel alarm clock. (I've finally discovered how to turn Mrs Bing-Bong off!)

09:00

Two days of visiting biblical sites in Turkey, Bethlehem and Jerusalem have just about dried up any remaining enthusiasm I may have had for taking any more excursions. Today, I'm going to chill out by the pool!

09:30

"Come and join the aerobics class, Anne – it'll be fun!" OB cries from her sunlounger.

"How come you're suddenly so interested in exercise? I don't suppose it's got anything to do with the instructor, has it?" I reply.

"Of course not!" she giggles, flapping her hands around her face as she speaks. (and I thought I was supposed to be the silly teenager!)

"I'll give it a miss, if you don't mind."

"Oh well, your loss!" she sulked. "Cooooey, Brian! Wait for me!"

Her high heels clatter as she totters towards the pool to join the class, her new silk kaftan (bought in Turkey) flowing behind her in the breeze. The heel of her shoe catches in a metal grid by the pool, causing her matching turban to fall over her sunglasses.   There is a deafening scream as she plunges into the pool.

09:31

I am too helpless with laughter to do anything to help as Brian dives into the pool and manages to grab hold of her.

13:45

OB's been sulking all morning. I can't stand this any longer - I'm going to have to do something about it.

"Hey, Mum. Shall we go and watch the film? They're showing your favourite."

"Which one?"

"Splash!"

"Very funny!"

The pain of her flip-flop hitting me in the head was worth making her laugh again – almost!

22:00

OB's mood seems even better now – It possibly has something to do with Brian fussing over her all evening!

"Ronnie, put your foot up on this sofa,"

"I don't think I can walk that far, Brian!"

"Don't worry, I'll carry you!"

She is soooo milking this!

Sunday 26 August

Why does no-one fancy me?

14:00

"I'm looking forward to the gala dinner tonight, aren't you?" OB asks as she applies more sun-tan lotion to her body.

"Not really, Mum." I reply, keeping my nose firmly stuck in my book.

"I'll do your hair and make-up for you – if you like."

"Whatever!"

I sigh and continue to read my book in the hope that she'll take the hint that she's boring me.

"You'll look lovely in that floral dress you chose."

"I didn't choose it – you did!"

"Well it'll look lovely anyway!"

"Fine! Can we stop talking about it now, please!"

I look up from my book and glare at her but she really doesn't seem to be taking the hint.

"I wonder if the captain will ask us to sit at his table?"

"Isn't that just for important people?"

"Hmmmm – We'll see…"

At last! She's shut up. Am sick of hearing about the Captain's Dinner. She's been on about it all day. What's the big deal anyway - it's just a stupid dinner?

19:30

"You are not seriously wearing that?!!!!" my jaw drops to the floor and my eyes bulge of their sockets in shock as OB walks out of the cabin washroom in what can only be described as a strip of black lace.

"Why? What's wrong with it?" she admires herself in the mirror. "I've got the figure for it!"

"It's like something one of those slapper girl bands would wear! Anyway, you're *way* too old to wear something like that!"

"How dare you call me a slapper!"

To my horror, she bursts into tears. I feel bad because I didn't mean to upset her. Now I'm over the shock, I can see that she does look good in the dress. It's just - SHE'S MY MUM!

"I didn't say that *you* were a slapper. It's just that the dress...well it's a bit full on isn't it? I mean, you're not even wearing undies!"

"Of course I am, you stupid girl! Have you never heard of flesh coloured thongs? I'm not likely to wear my Bridget Jones' under this am I?...Just grow up, Anne!"

21:30

I don't believe it! We walked through the door of the restaurant and the captain made a beeline for us and invited us

38

to sit at his table. I sat in silence through the whole meal as he talked to OB's boobs!

As the band starts to play, Brian approaches us. He seems to be trying to look right through mum's dress as he looks at her.

"You look...amazing!" he says as he looks her up and down.

"You don't look so bad yourself." She smiles, looking extremely pleased with herself.

He drags OB onto the dance floor and I'm left sitting on my own with a bunch of old fogies!

22:00

I'm still sat on my own. I swear that Brian's hands have not left my mum's backside since they started dancing!

22:30

OB's still on the dance floor, dancing with some bloke whose wife is giving her daggers! Brian's in a huff and has gone to the bar – at least he offered to buy me a drink!

23:00

I think Brian's got fed up of watching OB flirting with all the men who danced with her. He looks like some sort of brooding South American gaucho as he runs his hands through his dark hair and walks over to her and claims her back from some old bloke who was trying to cop a feel as they danced. – He's quite sexy when he's in a mood! They make a beautiful couple as they dance. Even I can see the chemistry as her slim blonde body moulds itself to his dark muscular frame. As for me? I'm fed up with waiting for someone to ask me to dance – I'm off to bed!

24:00

OB must be having a good time – she's not come back to our cabin yet.

02:00

Still not back.

03:00

Still not back – where has she got to?

04:30

Still not ....zzzzzzz

Monday 27 August

We're going home today – I can't wait to see Steph!

07:30

Woken by OB as she shut the cabin door.

"Where have you been?" I ask, sleepily.

"I couldn't sleep so I went for a walk up on deck."

"What time did you get back last night? I waited up for ages!"

"It was late – it must have been nearly three o'clock!"

"Oh, really?...So *you* enjoyed yourself last night," I said accusingly.

"Yes I did," she smiles.

Catching the sarcasm in my voice, OB sits on my bed and takes my hands. She gives me that look she always gives when she's about to give me a lecture.

"Look, darling, this holiday has been a wonderful experience for me. I've loved spending time with you...but I've also learned that I'm ready to claim back some of my own life. I've devoted the best part of twenty years to looking after your father...and you and your sisters."

"But, isn't that what mums are for?"

"I'm thirty–seven years old, Anne. I'm too young to fade away into the background. Your dad left five years ago. Your sisters have both left home. I need to make a life for myself

41

before *you* fly the nest too and leave me on my own! You're a big girl now so it's time for you to start growing up."

In other words - butt out Anne, I want to have some fun!

14:30

Hooray! We're on the flight home. OB's been a bit quiet since our "chat" this morning. She hardly said a word to me when we were packing our bags. I was mortified when Brian snogged her face off in front of the entire coach load of passengers before we left for the airport! She has spent most of the journey so far staring at a picture of Brian on her mobile.

15:00

The stewardess is starting to get stroppy with OB after telling her for the seventh time to switch her mobile off!

19:00

"I wonder if your sister remembered to put some fresh milk in the fridge? Be a love, Anne, and put the kettle on. I could murder a cup of tea!"

Home Sweet Home!

CHAPTER TWO

Back to School!

Saturday 8 September

I've spent most of my time since I got back from holiday with Steph. I can't see her today as I've been invited for lunch with Dad and Belinda (or The Bitch, as OB prefers to call her). I have promised Dad that I will try to be on my best behaviour but....

11:30

OB and me pull up outside Dad's house in her silver Yaris. I can tell she is seething when she spots the shiny red Audi TT parked next to Dad's Porche 911.

"I see The Bitch is at home then!" she smiles and pecks me on the cheek. "Have a nice time."

"See you later, Mum."

I bet The Bitch deliberately left that car in the drive just to show off to mum! Feel sorry for her as I stand on the pavement and watch her drive off.

11:31

"Anna, darling! Super to see you!" Belinda grabs hold of me, making silly Mwa! Mwa! sounds as she greets me with air kisses (I hate people who do that!) and takes me into the living room. "Did you have a lovely holiday?"

"What's it to you?" I scowl at her to remind her that we are never going to be friends.

"David! Are you going to let her talk to me like that?" she glares at Dad, who sighs as he gets out of his armchair to greet me.

"I've known this girl for over five years...and still I can't get a civil word out of her!" she whines.

Huh! She stole my Dad from under my mum's nose when she became a partner at the firm he works for six years ago. Dad's a solicitor (a senior partner). Mum says that, at some point, they confused the boardroom with the bedroom and never found their way back. And *she* expects me to be civil to her?

"Anne...sweetheart. Do you think we could get through just one visit without you acting like a spoilt brat?" Dad whispered as he gave me a hug.

Talking of brats – where are they? No sooner has the thought crossed my mind their presence is left in no doubt.

11:32

"Mummy!!" yells Brat number 1 (their five year old daughter, Olivia). "Joshua won't let me play with the Lego!"

"I'm coming darling!" Belinda scurries from the living room to the play room where the commotion is happening. "Now, Joshua, you must learn to play nicely."

It sounds like Brat number 1 has learned that she who shouts loudest gets what they want! I can hear the commotion as Belinda tries to persuade her two little darlings to play together.

"Ow! You naughty boy, Joshua!" I hear Belinda cry from the playroom. "How many times have I told you that hitting isn't nice? You can both stay in here until you apologise to me and learn to be nice to each other!"

Dad looks as though he is regretting starting a second family as Belinda returns to the living room holding her head, which has a nasty red mark on it where three year old Joshua (or Devil's Spawn, as I prefer to call him) has hit her over the head with a toy train.

17:00

I'm relieved as OB rescues me from the madhouse. At least I only have to visit once a month!

Monday 10 September

OB and I had a massive argument last night - probably something to do with me coming home drunk. O.K so it was her favourite rug, but she managed to clean the mess off it so I don't see why she has to make such a big deal of it!

My school-friend, Amber, found a bottle of wine in her mum's fridge so we decided to sneak it upstairs and drink it while we were doing our homework. Amber's great – not in a Steph way but I like her anyway. She's really pretty, with long blonde hair and the biggest blue eyes you've ever seen. All the boys at school act like idiots whenever she's around, so I can only guess that they must all fancy her something rotten. I, on the other hand, must be the obligatory ugly best mate – you know, the one that no-one fancies that all pretty girls seem to have tagging along with them to make them look even prettier!

In return for my "making someone who's already gorgeous look even more gorgeous" services, Amber helps me with my homework. I forgot to mention, she's really clever too! Me? Well I wasn't as far back in the cleverness queue as I was in the prettiness queue but I wasn't at the front either!

Anyway, I was a bit drunk when I got home last night from finishing the homework that we had been set for the summer holidays. OB was less than impressed when I made her favourite rug resemble a pavement pizza! She went ballistic and suddenly everything I had done wrong over the school holidays – in fact *ever* in my life – got thrown at me. From what I can remember, I stormed off to bed before she could say anymore.

07:30

My head feels like the Foo Fighters played a gig in it all night. I'm late for my first day back at school so I creep down to the kitchen, hoping to avoid OB and grab my school bag and go.

I almost retch as I can smell bacon and eggs being cooked. I'm not going to be able to get away with it. OB is in the kitchen, perfectly groomed in her designer clothes, high heels and apron. As she spots me, the kitchen turns into Nagsville!

"Baghdad doesn't look as messy as your bedroom."
"Yeah whatever! I'll probably split my sides at that one Mum – NOT!!"

"Eat your breakfast, Anne, it's the most important meal of the day."

I swear I'll scream if she says that one more time. She wouldn't be so keen on eating breakfast if she had a bum as big as mine. On second thoughts, she'd probably just use even *more* of her anti-cellulite creams and massage pads (or whatever else she keeps up in the bathroom!).

10:30

Things improved when I got to school - no really they did! Liam Grayson (he is soooo fit – he looks just like Johnny Depp!) sat next to me in maths – sigh!

16:30

The house has been a major ice zone since I've got home from school – I guess I'm not forgiven yet then!

Tuesday 11 September

I will try to avoid OB as much as possible today – maybe then I won't annoy her so much!

07:30

Got up late again this morning, much to OB's displeasure – I try to ignore a further nagging session as I eat my breakfast.

"You'll never make anything of yourself with this attitude."

"Whatever!"

"Is that all you can ever say for yourself?"

To make matters worse, OB insists on me doing the washing up. I mean, I thought that mums were supposed to look after you, not use you as slave labour!

11:00

Boo! Double English! I plonk my bag down on the floor next to my desk and wait for our teacher to arrive.

"I wonder who we've got this year?" asks Amber, who's sat next to me.

"Dunno - but they can't be much worse than Bossy Bains was last year!"

Our conversation is rudely interrupted by the classroom door being thrown open by Mr McCabe, the headmaster.

Hellooooo, who's that with him?

"Class 6a, I'd like to introduce you to a new member of staff, Mr Tom Price" Mr McCabe announces. "He will be your English teacher for this year. He's new to the school so I'm sure that I can rely on this class to show him how well-behaved the pupils of this school are."

Yessss! At last! We've got a buff teacher!

Mr McCabe leaves the room and our new teacher is left facing the class. He seems a little nervous as he addresses the class.

"As the headmaster has just informed you, my name is Mr Price."

OMG! He has got the sexiest voice ever! He sounds just like David Tennant! Somehow I don't think English is ever going to be boring again!

"I don't believe in running a stuffy classroom, so you can all call me Tom. As long as we all treat each other with respect, I think we'll all get on just fine!" he smiles at the class.

He is sooooo cool. English is definitely my favourite subject from now on!

13:00

Liam and his mates are looking over at me in the canteen. They are so obviously talking about me! To think I was ever interested in an immature boy like that!

Friday 14 September

Keeping out of OBs way seems to be doing the trick. At least she's not shouting at me any more! Even better, I'm sure Tom fancies me!

07:30

Yes! I've managed to get dressed before the alarm goes off. I've got plenty of time to make myself look good and sneak out of the house before OB can start nagging again!

12:30

Amber and me walk to the bakers at lunchtime and treat ourselves to a cream cake each. As cakes are banned from school (thanks very much Jamie Oliver!) we take them to the park and sit down on the grass to enjoy them.

12:32

OMG. Tom is walking across the grass towards us. He looks so cute in his Pringle sweater! (Hey, the retro 80s look is quite fashionable at the moment!) He approaches us just as I have taken a large bite out of my cream cake.

"Hello, Girls," he smiles. "How are you getting on with your essay on the similarities and differences between the book and film of Romeo and Juliet, Anne?"

"Fine thanks," I splutter after attempting to swallow as much of the mouthful as possible.

"Good...very good," he replies. "Well, I'll see you both in class. You know where I am if you need any help."

As he walks away, Amber bursts into hysterical laughter.

"You've got cream all over your nose and chin!" she points at my face with tears of laughter rolling down her cheeks.

I'm completely mortified. The cream cake has ruined my life! I'm never going to eat cream cake again.

18:00

I find myself daydreaming about Tom as I do my homework. Amber calls him a dork but I think she's just jealous that he smiled at me and not her! I think the grey in his hair looks distinguished. Okay, so his clothes need changing but I could always get him to buy some new ones. The tie with a fish on it and the tweed jacket with leather patches on his arms will certainly have to go – but the glasses are cute, even though you can't see his lovely grey eyes behind them – Sigh!!!

18:15

I conclude that the fact he asked me about homework - and *not* Amber - proves that he must fancy me. I start to practice my signature for when we get married.

Anne Price

Mrs Anne Price

Mrs A Price

18:30

I must concentrate on my homework. I don't want to let Tom down by not completing my essay.

Tuesday 18 September

Good things to happen today = invite to party (hooray!). Bad things to happen today = Tom not in school (boo!).

11:00

Yes! Double English!

Hang on? What's Mrs Jenkins doing here?

"No-one said she was taking class today. Where's Tom?" Amber whispers

"I don't know. I hope he's not ill."

12:30

English with Mrs Jenkins is sooooo dull. I hope Tom comes back soon.

13:00

Amber, Sarah Smithers (only the most popular girl in school) and me are trying to decide whose parents are more stupid. Their mums have got nothing on OB!

"I got a new CD at the weekend. It's really wicked!! OB, who reckons she is such a liberated mum, thought that Primal Scream was some sort of ancient mating call or something – God she can be soooo stupid sometimes!!"

"Okay, you win!" Sarah laughs.

Yes! I made the most popular girl in school laugh. I must be on way to being accepted by her!

16:00

Sarah catches up with Amber and me as we walk home from school.

"Amber!"

Amber stops walking as soon as we hear her voice. Apparently, it's not the done thing to make Sarah run after you!

"Have you told Anne about my party on Saturday?"

"No Sarah, I didn't know that you wanted to invite her."

"Of course I do! You'll come won't you, Anne?"

"Well, I..."

"Seven-thirty. You know where I live. Be there!" she orders and then walks away.

Wow! Sarah Smithers actually just invited me to her party! – how cool is that!!!

18:00

I am in a state of panic as I realize that I've got nothing suitable to wear on Saturday. I'm going to have to try to persuade OB to take me shopping on Saturday morning.

18:01

On second thoughts, I'll probably ask OB for money and go shopping with Amber!

Wednesday 19 September

Tom's wife had a baby yesterday – I WANT TO DIE!!!!

Saturday 22 September

I've been too upset to write diary for past three days. I hate Tom!

10:00

I'm not going to the party tonight. My eyes are all red and puffy from crying all night. How could he have a baby? How dare he have a WIFE!

11:00

There's no way I could go to the party even if I wanted to as OB wouldn't let me buy any new clothes.

"You've got plenty of clothes in your wardrobe."

"Yes, but nothing that wouldn't get me laughed out of Sarah's house!"

"Don't be so vain, young lady! There are people in the world that would kill to have a wardrobe full of clothes like you."

"Whatever!"

"For goodness sake, Anne. Just lately you seem to have developed a one word vocabulary – whatever." (said in a sarcastic tone).

11:30

I just looked at myself in the mirror and I've got a spot under my chin bigger than Mount Everest - and bags under my eyes that could hold mum's weekly shopping. Definitely not a good look!

Talking of bags, OB has been quite sweet since I told her about Tom. How did she know how I was feeling? She even tidied my room for me – WEIRD!

16:30

Liam just telephoned me and asked if he could take me to the party – maybe he's not so bad after all!

17:00

Just remembered I've got nothing to wear! Will have to phone Liam and tell him I can't go to party!

17:45

I'm going to party after all! Mum lent me one of her new dresses (not the black lace thing!). It's a really cool retro psychedelic mini dress that will look fab with my white boots - so I didn't need to phone Liam and cancel.

Better get a move on 'cos I've got less than an hour and a half to wash my hair and put my slap on before Liam picks me up!

19:15

He's here! I stand in my bedroom panicking. Do I look alright? What if I look too fat in this dress! Liam won't fancy me and I'll be a laughing stock with the girls!

"Anne! Liam's here" OB calls from the hallway.

"Just coming!"

I can see Liam from the top of the stairs. He's standing at the front door with his back to me. I take a deep breath and pray that I don't fall as I walk down the stairs.

"Wow! You look awesome!" Liam's face lights up as he turns round and sees me.

Suddenly going out with Johnny Depp doesn't seem such a bad idea!

Sunday 23 September

Liam asked me round to his house to watch a DVD of "Pirates of the Caribbean - Dead Man's Chest" tonight. (I'll be seeing double!). Will have to go to Steph's first though to tell her all about it. I am in lurve!!!

08:00

I'm still singing to myself as I walk into the kitchen. I feel so mature now that I've got a boyfriend, I think to myself as I help myself to a bowl of coco pops. I feel extremely pleased with myself as I polish off the bowl in record time.

"Mum, I'm going round to Steph's today and then I'm going to Liam's. We're having pizza so I won't be back for dinner."

"Okay, but don't be too late – You've got school in the morning!"

I smile and nod at her before licking the last of the chocolate milk from the bottom of the bowl – I thought love was supposed to suppress the appetite!"

"What, no arguments? Someone's in a good mood this morning!"

"I'm in lurve! – Liam's soooo cool!" I sigh.

"I thought you were in *luuurve* with Tom!" OB laughs.

"Nah! That was just kids' stuff! – This is the real thing!" I tell her as I peck her on the cheek and run to the back door. "See you later!"

She has the strangest smile on her face as I leave the house. I'll never understand her.

10:00

"Steph, the party was brilliant! Sarah's Mum and Dad are really ace. They went out for the evening so we could enjoy the party in the absence of wrinklies!"

"I'm glad you enjoyed yourself...I saw a good film on TV last night..." she replies.

"Their house is amazing! The party was in their conservatory...I mean, can you believe it, a conservatory big enough to hold a party in? I've never seen one as big as that ...It's sooooo massive! I think it might actually be bigger than our entire house!

"Really? I've never been invited to a posh party like that!... In fact I've never been invited to a party anywhere...well not since I was five anyway!"

"You'd have loved it...everyone was there."

"Not quite everyone..."

"Sarah's friends are soooo cool. Mind you, I could actually feel pretty smug...because I was there with, like, the coolest boy in the whole school! I definitely earned a new respect from Amber and her friends...even though I could tell they were also a bit jealous!"

"Good for you!"

"Sorry, am I going on a bit?"

"No, No...you carry on! It's not like I'm likely to have anything exciting to tell you...like parties or boyfriends or..."

"Okay. Well, some of the others got really drunk and threw up in the garden. I bet Mrs Smithers wasn't too pleased when she found that this morning!...I hope Sarah doesn't get into too much trouble!"

"I was actually being sarcastic...I'm getting pretty bored of Sarah's party now!"

"Oh, right. Well I'll just tell you the best bit then. Liam kissed me when the slow dances started at the end of the party. A full on snog!! Actually, it was a bit sloppier than I imagined it would be."

"Gross!"

"Still I'm happy now that I've had my first proper snog!!

13:30

Steph seemed a bit narky with me earlier. Can't think why. Oh well! If she wants to get a moody on just because I've got a boyfriend that's her business! Got to go now as I don't want to be late for Liam.

13:45

I arrive at Liam's house. I feel really nervous as I press the doorbell and want to turn back in case it was all a dream and I've made a complete fool of myself. OMG I can see him coming through the glass in the door.

"Hi."

"Hi."

We both stand there grinning at each other for what seems like ages before he asks me in.

13:47

Liam didn't tell me we'd be watching the DVD in his bedroom! I'm not sure what OB would say if she knew about this.

13:48

Actually – I *do* know what OB would say if she knew about this…so I won't be telling her!

16:30

"Dead Man's Chest" just finished on the TV. I didn't catch much of it as I was too busy snogging my very own Jack Sparrow! The bits I did see looked quite good though – maybe Steph and I can watch it some other time!

"I'm starving!" Liam jumps up from his bed. "I'll get us a drink and then we can order pizza. Here! Choose the one you want!" he throws a leaflet from the local pizza house at me and disappears from the room.

20:00

I get home after having a perfect day. I got to spend time with my best friend and then Johnny Depp and pepperoni pizza with my fantastic new boyfriend – what more could a girl want?

I go to my room to practice my new signature for when Liam and I get married.

Anne Grayson

Mrs Anne Grayson

Mrs A Grayson

Monday 24 September

Watch out school – here comes the woman with a boyfriend!

07:30

I can't wait to go to school and see Liam. Everyone will know by now that we are an item!

09:15

I'm sure everyone's looking at me differently. They must all know. I give them all my best smug smile (in case they don't know) – then they will wonder what I'm being so smug about and I will be forced to tell them – I'VE GOT A BOYFRIEND!

16:00

I haven't seen much of Liam today – I wonder if he's avoiding me?

16:01

Ah, there he is! He's over by the school gate, talking to his two best friends, Gareth and Jack. I wonder if he's telling them about me? I'd best go and find out.

16:02

They haven't seen me yet. I try to adopt an air of nonchalance as I approach them.

"I've got to hand it to you mate – I almost feel sorry for you," Gareth laughs as he hands Liam a ten pound note.

"Yeah, me too! I never thought you'd actually manage to pull the moose!" Jack handed over another ten pounds.

I feel sick! How could he do this to me? He asked me to the party for a bet!!! I walk away as fast as I can, hoping that he hasn't seen me.

"Anne! I can explain!..." I hear Liam cry as he spots me.

I don't want to hear any more. Tears burn my cheeks as I run all the way home. I'm never going to be able to show my face in school again!!!

16:15

Good - OB isn't in. I run upstairs to my bedroom and fling myself onto my bed. What's wrong with me? Why does no-one fancy me? - A moose! That's what they called me – A MOOSE!

17:00

I weigh myself on the bathroom scales - eight stone eight lbs. Is that good? I've no idea!

17:01

I switch on my computer and look for a weight chart on the internet. Aha! Found one!

Women
Five feet four inches
eight stone eight pounds

OMG - I'm almost overweight! I'm not just a moose – I'm virtually a hippopotamus!

No wonder Liam doesn't really fancy me! I'm starting a diet immediately.

Tuesday 25 September

LIAM IS A PIG! I HATE HIM!!

Saturday 29 September

School this week has been a nightmare! I've been too ashamed to speak to anyone and hid myself in the library at lunchtime so no-one would find me. Depression is good for the diet though – I've lost 3 lbs - eight stone five pounds!

10:30

"Anne! Your father's on the phone…he wants to speak to you!"

I get up from sofa and OB hands me the phone. She takes my place on the sofa and I sit in her arm-chair to take the call.

"Hello?"

"Hello, Darling. How's my number one girl today?"

"What did you want, Dad?"

"Belinda and I were wondering if you were busy today?"

"Not really, why?"

"I need to take Belinda shopping and I was wondering if you would come and look after Olivia and Josh for a couple of hours…be an angel and say yes!"

"Can Steph come too?"

"Yes of course!"

"Okay, what time?"

"Can you be here in an hour?"

"Fine! – Bye!"

11:30

OB drops Steph and me at Dad's. I have briefed Steph about the brats on the way but I'm not sure even that will prepare her for an afternoon with them two!

11:45

After giving us an extensive list of do's and don'ts, Belinda and Dad have finally gone! Steph and me settle down on the sofa to watch some TV.

"Waaaaaaah!" Brat number One screams from the play room.

"Ignore her," I say to Steph. "She's just attention seeking!"

"Waaaaaaah! – Josh give me back my dolly!!"

"Shouldn't we go and sort them out?" asks Steph.

"You can if you like – but I'm telling you, it's dangerous in there!"

11:46

"Come along now Josh, give your sister her dolly back – there's a good boy…ow! You little…"

Steph returns to the living room rubbing her shin where Josh has kicked her.

14:00

I have now got a major headache from all the screaming coming from the next room so I decide it's time for their afternoon nap. Olivia screams all the way up the stairs as Steph tries to persuade her to go up to her room. Josh nearly kicks me black and blue as I attempt to get him up the stairs without him killing me.

14:15

"Waaaaaah! Wanna come down and play!" screams Brat number One.

We run up the stairs. I narrowly avoid major injury as I trip on one of Josh's toy trains.

"I'm sure that wasn't there when we brought them up here!" I say as I pick it up.

"Where's it come from then?" asked Steph.

"Devil's Spawn!" I reply knowingly. "He's trying to kill me!"

"Don't be silly, he's only three! Even *he* can't be that evil!" Steph gasps in astonishment.

We look into his bedroom. He looks so angelic as he sleeps. I shudder as I reply,

"I wouldn't be so sure, Steph!"

16:00

The house is quiet but I'm still traumatised by thoughts of my half-brother trying to kill me. Dad and Belinda return from their shopping trip. She looks like the cat that's got the cream as she walks over to us and flashes a huge diamond ring on her left hand.

"Your father and I are getting married!" she shrieks as she waggles her newly manicured fingers to show off the giant stone.

"Belinda! I wanted to be the one to tell her the good news!" Dad shot me an apologetic look as he spoke.

"Sorry, I couldn't wait...I'm soooo excited. Just wait 'til you see the bridesmaid's dress I've picked out for you, Anne. You'll love it!"

Bridesmaid! Me? There's no way I'm walking down the aisle behind her!

"Dad, I can't be your bridesmaid...Mum would never forgive me!"

Clever move, using Mum as an excuse.

"She's bound to be a bit upset at first...but she'll come round. Please sweetheart, it would mean so much to me," he looks at me with pleading eyes.

"I'll think about it."

"Good girl!" he says as he puts his arms around me to give me a hug.

17:00

I'm in a no win situation. Either I agree to be a bridesmaid and make Dad happy (which would really upset OB) or refuse to be a bridesmaid and please my mum – but hurt Dad's feelings.

Why do parents have to make life so difficult?

CHAPTER THREE

The Royal Family

Saturday 6 October

I've decided that I don't want a boyfriend. I'm working on improving my image instead. Diet is going v well – Eight stone two – total weight loss of six pounds! Still look like a hippo though!

11:00

A knock at the front door turns out to be my oldest sister, Elizabeth. She's 18 and dropped out of university earlier this year when she fell pregnant with her daughter Lilly. Her drippy boyfriend, Nathan, married her when Lilly was born. He's still a student so they've got no money and the three of them live in a grotty bed-sit in Brighton.

"Mum!" she sobs as OB stands aside to let her in.

Elizabeth's long curly dark hair is shoved casually up into a woolly hat, which Lilly grabs hold of and pulls off her head as she steps through the door with Lilly in one arm and a suitcase in the other. Even when she's upset, Elizabeth still looks beautiful. She has a natural beauty, and never needs make-up to look good. She's got the same dark eyes as Dad (although they look a bit bloodshot at the moment from crying!) and a lovely smile (again not evident at this precise moment!).

"I never want to see him again!" she wails.

"Put the kettle on, Anne while I help Elizabeth take her things into the living room...there's a good girl!"

In other words, make yourself scarce, Anne...we've got adult things to talk about!

12:00

I figure that OB and Elizabeth have had long enough to talk and take some tea and sandwiches into the living room. Lilly is asleep on the sofa next to Elizabeth, who seems to have cheered up a bit.

"Thanks Sis," Elizabeth manages a smile as she helps herself to a cheese and cucumber sandwich (see, I even remembered she's vegetarian – that's the sort of caring sister I am!)

"Elizabeth and Lilly are going to be staying for a while," explains OB. "She and Nathan are having a few problems, but I'm sure it's nothing that a few days apart won't solve."

15:00

"Don't babies do anything other than sleep? I ask Elizabeth as we watch Lilly, who is still asleep on the sofa.

"Other than cry, eat and soil their nappies...not a lot," she laughs as she strokes Lilly's face with her finger tips.

"I think I'll give babies a miss."

"Well at least for a while, eh?...Have your heard anything from Mags lately?"

Mags is our other sister, well her name's Margaret really. OB always did think she was a cut above everyone else and named us all after the royal family! Mags is the fiery, adventurous one of the family (typical of a curly red-head) and is currently away travelling the world on a gap year from university.

"Not for a while," I reply. "Last I heard, she was staying in some sort of hippie commune in Goa."

We only get a post card when she moves from one place to another. The house seems pretty quiet without her as she and OB have been known to have some proper blazing rows when Mags gets herself into one scrape or another.

"That sounds like Mags!"

Sunday 7 October

Elizabeth and Lilly seem to have settled in well. OB went to Elizabeth's flat to fetch Lilly's cot for her – I think she secretly wanted to let Nathan know that his wife and daughter were OK.

09:30

I can hear Nathan at the front door talking to Mum.

"Please, Ronnie, I just want to talk to her."

"I'm sorry, Nathan, but I don't think she wants to speak to you right now. Why don't you give her a few days to calm down?"

"It's Okay, Mum, let him in," Elizabeth calls from the living room.

OB and me sit in the kitchen, drinking a cup of tea while they talk.

09:45

Elizabeth and Nathan started off talking quietly but OB starts to look worried as their voices are raised and we can hear their arguing.

"I left you because you're a lazy, selfish, good-for-nothing waster, who would rather sit around, playing with your Play-Station, than go out to work to provide for your wife and child...is that clear enough for you? Lilly and I are not stepping foot back in that dump!"

"Well if it's a dump, it's because you don't clean it! All you do all day is look after a baby! I'm trying to finish my degree…I didn't ask to be landed with a wife and a baby while I'm trying to study!"

"Fine! If that's how you feel, but I'm warning you, we're not coming back until you get a job and somewhere decent to live!

"Fine!"

The front door slams as Nathan storms out of the house.

12:00

I'm fed up with listening to Elizabeth blubbing to Mum about Nathan. I think I will make myself scarce and go round to Amber's to do homework.

15:30

"Thanks for helping with the algebra, Amber. I don't think I could have done it without you."

"That's Okay. Do you want something to drink?" Amber flicks her blonde hair as she stands up from the kitchen table.

"Just water please, I'm on a diet." I replied, feeling pleased with myself for not being tempted to ask for cola.

"I thought you'd lost weight!" she grins as she pours us some fizzy water.

"Thanks!" I say, in response to both the compliment and to the glass of water she hands me.

"I hope you're not doing this for Liam's benefit?"

"As if!" I scoff.

"Well, good for you!" Amber raises her glass to me. "You look much better already!"

Yes! Have vision of me being accepted into the group because I look good, rather than for being ugly friend who makes all the others look pretty.

Wednesday 10 October

I'm feeling really good today – I've lost ten pounds! At this rate I should turn into Kate Moss by Xmas!

07:45

Postcard from Mags (Hooray!)

Dear Mum and Sis,

We've decided to drag ourselves away from Goa before we've chilled out so much that we forget we are supposed to be travelling! We've had a fab time here. The culture is so different. I've taken loads of photos so be prepared to be bored stiff by them when we get home!

JB, (her boyfriend – she met him at Uni. OB doesn't like him) *fancies Israel next, so we're off to find work on a Kibbutz. Will write again when we get there!*

Miss you loads!

Love Mags

p.s. give my love to Elizabeth, Nathan and Lilly when you see them.

I'd forgotten how much I miss Mags!

10:00

Liam has been looking at me all through Maths! I wonder what he wants? Oh no, he's coming over!

"Hi."

"What do you want, Liam?" I push the chair back from my desk and stand up.

"I understand if you're still mad at me..."

"Talk to the hand 'cos the face ain't list'ning!" I hold the palm of my hand out in front of him and look away from him with my nose in the air to demonstrate my snub.

Hah! I can hear some of our class mates giggling at him as I strut out of the classroom.

10:30

If Liam thinks he can worm his way back with me just as I'm about to become a supermodel, he's got another think coming!

11:00

I'll give him Moose!

Saturday 13 October

We don't get visitors for months and suddenly the house becomes a drop-in centre!

11:00

The front doorbell rings and I get half way down the stairs as OB answers the door. OB looks as though she's seen a ghost when she sees who's standing on the doorstep.

"Brian!"

I think she's going to faint.

"Hi, Ronnie!"

What's *he* doing here? Look at him, standing at the door grinning at her as if he were doing her some sort of favour just being here (sun-tanned and gorgeous though he may be!).

"What are you doing here? I mean...you haven't been in touch since I left Rhodes!"

Poor Mum! Not one reply to her text messages in seven weeks - and he turns up here expecting her to be happy to see him. He's got a cheek!

"You know how it is, Ron," he shrugs. "You don't get a minute to yourself on that ship. I missed you though!" He pouts his bottom lip out and hold his arms out to her.

Yeah, right! More like the other poor saps on your list of conquests refused to take you in and you haven't got anywhere else to stay!

"You could have at least let me know you were coming!"

Ha! He's in trouble now! I recognize that tone!

"I though it'd be nice to surprise you...well aren't you going to ask me in? I've travelled a long way to come and see you."

Mum, you are not seriously going to fall for that one are you? Oh no! He's looking at her with puppy-dog eyes. I think she's weakening!

"Well, I suppose a few minutes won't hurt," OB opens the door wider so Brian and his suitcases can get through the door.

Well done, Mum! That told him!!

14:30

OB is an idiot! She's been all over him since he arrived. I've lost all respect for woman who obviously has none for herself! I can't wait for Elizabeth to get back from taking Lilly to see Nathan. Maybe she can talk some sense into her.

15:45

"Hi Sis!"

Elizabeth is back! She lets herself in the back door. I'm in the middle of making a pot of tea (the fourth lot that OB has sent me into the kitchen to make – much more of this and he'll think I'm some sort of room service!). I break away to help Elizabeth lift Lilly's buggy over the step, into the kitchen.

"You're an angel," she says as we place the buggy in the middle of the floor. "Oh good, you're making tea...I could do with a cup!"

"Okay, grab an extra cup while I pour these."

Elizabeth reaches up into the cupboard and takes her favourite china mug from the shelf. She peers through the door into the living room and spots Brian.

"Who's He?" she mouths as she hands her mug to me.

"Brian," I whisper. "The one she met on holiday!"

"Way to Go Mum!...He's drop dead gorgeous!" she whispered, her mouth gaping open.

"Yeah well, when you put your tongue away, you might just see what a creep he is!"

"What do you mean?"

She listens while I tell her the situation (well as much as I can manage before the tea stews).

"Hmmmm, I see what you mean," she replies. "We'll have to keep an eye on him...and Mum for that matter!"

You don't stand a chance now, Brian! We'll be watching your every move!

Sunday 14 October

Brian's moved his things straight into OB's bedroom. They didn't even have the decency to pretend that he was sleeping on the sofa. He's soooo obviously having sex with my mum!

08:30

OB and Brian are sat at the kitchen table eating breakfast as I wander into the kitchen. I feel physically sick as I watch them gaze at each other while they butter their toast. I grab my mini box of Special K and sit at the table in between them. I glare at them to show my disapproval. Honestly! It's enough to put me off as I pour a splash of semi-skimmed milk onto the measly portion.

08:31

I eat my cereal in silence. I've never known OB not to get dressed before coming down for breakfast. She's normally perfectly groomed and in full make-up before she sets foot out of her bedroom. Today, she's sat in her silk dressing-gown with her hair all tussled. She might as well be wearing a sign saying "Me and Brian have been having sex!" Gross!

09:00

I can't stand being in the same house as those two for a minute longer! I'm going round to Steph's.

10:00

Steph and me sit on her bed listening to my Primal Scream CD as I tell her about OB and Brian. She is suitably unimpressed.

"NEWSFLASH, MUM" I say as a dramatic finale to my tale of depravity (note to Tom – see, I *can* use the word

91

depravity in a proper sentence!). "MUMS DON'T HAVE SEX!!!

"You poor thing!" Steph replies, sympathetically. (I knew I could count on Steph to understand).

"I know!" I say dramatically (I'm liking all this sympathy – I think I will milk it for a little bit longer!)

"I don't think my mum and dad have *ever* had sex." Steph says in all seriousness.

"Duh! They had *you* didn't they?" I laugh

"Well, maybe they only had sex the once!" she replied indignantly.

"That would make sense," I nod gravely. "They probably didn't want to risk making the same mistake again!"

I'm hilarious! I collapse in hysterics at my own geniusly witty response.

"Kill her Missie!" Steph shouts at her cat, who has been curled up asleep on her pillow since I arrived

Missie stands up unsteadily on the pillow and gives a huge yawn. As I watch the normally docile English Blue exposing her vicious looking teeth, she actually looks like she might obey Steph and attack me. I sigh with relief when she just gives us a disapproving stare and pads the pillow with her paws before settling down to go back to sleep.

"Oh well," sighs Steph. "It was worth a try!"

Tuesday 16 October

This house is too small for five!

08:00

I slam the front door as I leave for school. I'm well fed up! Why is it that, just because I'm the youngest, I'm always the last to get to use the bathroom? I'm the only one who actually had anywhere to be this morning, yet I ended up having to wash my hair in lukewarm water! It's soooo unfair!

09:00

History is DULL. So a bunch of people lived before us and had wars and a bunch of other stuff – So what's new? Get over it! BORING!

12:30

"Sarah and me wondered if you'd like to come round to mine tonight to watch Pirates of the Caribbean: At World's End." Amber asks as we walk into the school canteen for lunch. (It's raining outside and we can't be bothered to go out anywhere for lunch.)

"I don't DO Johnny Depp films any more!"

"Ooops! Sorry, I forgot!" she grins. "We can watch something else, if you like."

They are actually prepared to watch a different film to please *me*? Hooray! I have obviously been properly accepted into Sarah's circle of friends.

18:00

Seven and a half stones! Fantastic – have lost almost a stone in weight. Will allow myself celebratory Mars Bar tomorrow – or similar.

18:01

Am fed up! Just looked in the mirror and backside still resembles the back of a bull elephant! Mars Bar will have to wait. I definitely need to step up the diet.

18:15

"Hi, Sis!"

Elizabeth pokes her head round my bedroom door.

"Hi!"

"Can I come in?"

"Sure!"

She looks a bit sheepish as she walks into my room and sits on my bed.

"I've come to say goodbye," she smiles. "Nathan and me have decided to give it another go. He's got a bar job three nights a week...and he says he's cleaned the flat. I'm taking Lilly back there now."

"But what about Mum and Brian? You can't leave me on my own with them!"

"I'll be right on the end of the phone if you need me. I can be here in next to no time!" she smiles as she gives me a hug. "Bye, Sis."

"Bye!"

I watch as she leaves my room. Will definitely miss having my big sister around.

18:30

I'm still a bit sad as I leave to go to Amber's house. I wonder what film I should choose?

Wednesday 17 October

I think I might have lost a few brownie points with Amber and Sarah last night.

It turns out that they had invited Abigail and India around to watch the film as well as me. They don't seem to have much of a sense of humour so maybe Shrek 2 wasn't the best choice of film!

I tried to amuse them all with my impressions of "Donkey" but they stared at me with a look of horror on their faces. I'm sure I saw India and Abi smirking when they thought I wasn't looking. Steph would definitely have found it funny!

Have learned my lesson and now know that that if I want to have more sophisticated friends then I must stop having fun. I can only hope that I haven't damaged my chances of another invite!

06:30

Feel smug as I get up early this morning to get to the bathroom before the others.

07:15

Damn! I forgot Elizabeth isn't here any more so I'm already dressed for school. I decide to make breakfast for OB and Brian by way of apology for being sulky with them. I must try and get on with Brian for Mum's sake.

07:45

"Is this margarine on my toast?" Brian lifts a piece of toast to inspect it.

"Yes. Is that a problem?" I smile sweetly.

97

"I don't eat anything synthetic!" he sniffs and pushes the toast away from him.

I grit my teeth and try very hard not to say anything about him being ungrateful.

"This orange juice isn't freshly squeezed! You've given me that supermarket rubbish!" he splutters as he sips from the glass of juice I had put in front of him. "My body is a temple! You know I don't eat or drink anything that isn't fresh!"

"Sorry!" I mutter.

07:46

Scrub thoughts of trying to get on with Brian. He is an ungrateful pig! Who does he think he is, coming in here and making demands about what food and drink he's given? I don't recall him putting his hand in his pocket to buy any of it!

09:00

"Hi, Amber!"

"Oh, Hi!"

She's smiling so that's a good sign.

"Sorry if I embarrassed you yesterday…you know with the "Donkey" impressions."

"Actually, I thought they were quite funny!" she laughed. "But it's probably best if you don't do them in front of that lot again. Bit un-cool…if you know what I mean!"

I'm glad Amber is my friend. I must try to be more like her in future!

Saturday 20 October

I've saved up enough pocket money to go on shopping spree to Brighton! My old clothes are too naff to be seen out in with Amber and my new friends.

09:00

"I'll come shopping with you, if you like," offered Steph. "I need a new pair of trainers anyway!"

"Oh, no. It's okay," I lie. "OB's decided that she wants us to have a girly shopping trip together...you know how it is!"

"Oh right," she sounds disappointed. "Maybe I'll see you later then."

"Yeah, maybe. We can have a laugh at the tragic clothes OB makes me buy!"

"Okay, I'll see ya later then!"

"Yeah, see ya!"

I cringe with guilt as I put the phone receiver down.

09:01

I don't feel good about lying to Steph but – the truth is, Amber has already promised to come with me and I'd rather go shopping with her. Well, Steph's hardly a fashion guru! I only told her a white lie so I suppose what she doesn't know won't hurt her!

15:00

I'm having the best day out shopping with Amber and Sarah. I picked out three mega-cool tops. I've decided to go for a contemporary rock chick look.

"Eat your heart out K T Tunstall!" I cry as we walk into New Look to find some jeans to go with my new tops. We head for the rails and start to inspect the jeans.

"Oh my God! Major Geek Alert!" sneers Sarah as she points over to something over by the shoe section.

"Now that...is what you call sad!" agrees Amber as they burst into fits of giggles.

My gaze follows the line of Sarah's finger to see who it is they are laughing at.

"Steph!" I gasp.

"What?" they both ask.

"Def- in -itely the winner of Geek of the Week!" I reply.

"Geek of the Week!...That's really funny, Anne!" Amber laughs out loud.

Oh, No! Steph just looked over and has spotted me out with my friends. The look of hurt on her face is crushing. I don't know whether she actually heard us dissing her or if she is just hurt because she knows I lied to her about going shopping with Mum. Either way, I feel ashamed as she walks out of the shop.

Tuesday 23 October

Steph hasn't rung me. I feel bad about hurting her. I must try to think of way to make it up to her.

07:45

Hooray! Another postcard from Mags!

Hi Mum and Sis,

Sorry I haven't had a chance to write before now but I had a spot of bother when I first got to Israel. JB got arrested when he got caught smuggling a lump of black through customs in Israel. Don't worry, I was released after a few hours when I convinced them that I didn't know anything about it. I wasn't allowed to go anywhere until they made up their minds what they were going to do with JB. They deported him two days ago!

Would you believe he actually thought I should cut my holiday short to come back with him? As if! I've dumped him instead and have decided to travel on with Maddie and Sian, two Welsh girls that I met in the hostel I stayed in after leaving JB. We made it to the Kibbutz yesterday. I like it here, the work's hard but the people seem really friendly.

Love you both!

Mags

"I knew I should never let her go!" OB starts to panic as she finishes reading the postcard. "Trouble seems to follow that girl wherever she goes!"

"She'll be fine, Mum," I squeeze her hand. "You know Mag's...she falls into a bag of manure and always seems to come out smelling of roses...she's never been beaten by anything yet!"

"I hope you're right." she sighs.

11:00

Mrs Jenkins has just told us that Tom is coming back from his paternity leave after half term. No offence to the boring old cow, but English just hasn't been the same without him!

17:00

As part of my new image, Amber promised to dye my hair. I look at my hair for the last time in the mirror. It's sooo boring! Neither blonde nor brown, just a mousy sort of beige!

"Here we go!" Amber sings as she mixes the powder and bottle of liquid in a plastic tray. "This blonde is really going to suit you!"

"Argh! That's cold!" I yelp as the first of the gooey mixture hits my head.

"Stop being a baby. We all have to suffer for beauty!"

"Are you sure you know what you're doing?"

"Of course! I've done it loads of times," she replies.

I sit and patiently let her apply the rest of the mixture to my hair with a brush. My nose wrinkles at the smell. I swear I can feel my head burning!

17:30

"Is it supposed to sting like this?" I ask as Amber checks the colour for the fiftieth time.

"It doesn't look very blonde yet, but we'd better rinse it off if it really is stinging you," she replies.

We rush to her bathroom where Amber rinses the slime off my hair with a shower head as I bend over the bath. My head feels like it's on fire by the time we get back to her room.

"Well? What does the colour look like? I ask her.

"Erm, it's not exactly the colour I thought it would be," she grimaces.

"ARGH!!!!!! I look like my head's been Tango'd!" I scream as I look in the mirror at the orange blob of hair on top of my head.

"It might look better after we dry it!" Amber suggests hopefully as she grabs her hairdryer.

"Well it can't look any worse!" I howl.

Amber starts to dry my hair with the hairdryer but the heat burns my head so badly that I can't stand the pain. Turning the dryer off, Amber looks at my scalp.

"Ouch!" she winces. "It's covered in blisters!....I suppose we should have done the test patch before using the dye."

17:45

Amber runs into her brother, Harry's, room and pinches one of his hats.

"It's okay," she insists. "He doesn't wear this one any more so he's not likely to miss it."

"I look like Ronald McDonald!" I wail as I pull the black beret over my orange hair.

18:30

I creep into the house, hoping to get upstairs before OB or Brian sees me.

"Anne? Is that you?" OB calls from the living room as I attempt to sneak past.

"Yes, Mum," I reply and carry on towards the stairs.

"What the hell…"

"Damn! She's seen it!"

I turn to face her and burst into tears when I see the look of horror on her face.

21:00

Something is definitely not right! My head and face are both burning now. I decide that I'm going to have to take another look at myself in the mirror.

OMG! I look like a beetroot and carrot salad. My face is bright red and swollen and my scalp is the same colour.

"Mum! I yell …can you come here please?"

Saturday 27 October

I've been too traumatised to even think about Steph! She still hasn't called – she really must be having a major strop!

After OB had seen the damage to my head and face, she called the doctor, who confirmed that I had suffered a severe allergic reaction to the hair dye. I've been off school for the last three days, with my face and head covered in various ointments. It's been horrible! My skin is now more like the colour of cooked prawn than beetroot - but at least the swelling has almost gone.

OB has been really nice to me. She's even asked her friend, Beverley (who owns the most amazing hairdressers in Brighton) to come round later to see if she can do anything about my hair.

09:00

"Anne! Come down love, Elizabeth's here to see you."

"I'm not seeing anyone while I look like this!"

"For goodness sake! She's not *anyone*…she's your sister!"

I ignore her and pull the duvet back over my head. I'm not getting up until I have to get ready for Beverley to sort out the mess.

09:05

"Hey, Sis…it's me." Elizabeth knocks my bedroom door. "Can I come in?"

"Go away!"

"I just want to see how you are."

"You'll just laugh at me!"

"No I won't …I promise!"

"Alright …but if you laugh I'll never speak to you again!"

09:06

I am NEVER speaking to her again! She took one look at me and burst into hysterics. I will never be able to show my face in public again!

10:00

"Actually, with a good cut, that colour could really work," Beverley said as she studied me.

"No way! I'm not staying this colour!" I wail.

"Your skin is too delicate to put any more chemicals near your scalp. The only options you've got are to leave it as it is or to make the colour work for you."

"Darling, Bev knows what she's doing. She's been good enough to come here this morning. The least you can do is let her try and help you."

"I s'pose so," I reply doubtfully.

11:00

"Wow! I look sooooooo cool!"

I admire my new haircut in the mirror. Beverley washed my hair and spent ages cutting my shoulder length hair into a trendy new short asymmetric bob. Instead of looking mingin', the bright orange looks really wicked!

"Thanks Bev, you're a genius!" I grin.

"You're welcome," she smiles.

Sunday 28 October

Brian goes back to the ship today – Hooray!!

08:00

Yessss! Seven stone five! Will definitely give Kate Moss a run for her money by Xmas!

08:01

Nooooo! There must be something wrong with the bathroom scales! I've just looked in the mirror and even with my excellent new haircut, I still look like a fat pig! Must try harder with my diet or will never look like Amber and Sarah!

11:00

I take a deep breath as I ring the doorbell at Steph's. Her mum answers the door.

"Hi, is Steph in?" I ask nervously.

"Yes, who shall I say is calling?"

"It's me! Anne!" I know I've got orange hair, but her mum doesn't seem to recognize me.

"Good God! So it is!" she seems taken aback as she lets me in. Duh! I've only been coming round here for the last ten years!

11:01

"Blimey!" Steph stares at me as I walk through her bedroom door. "You look so different!"

Missie opens an eye from her usual spot in the middle of Steph's pillow. When she sees it's me, she "chirrups" and stands up to stretch her body before slinking across the bed to greet me. She purrs loudly as she rubs her body around my jeans.

"Well at least someone's pleased to see me!" I smile as I pick Missie up to fuss her. "Look, Steph, I'm really sorry I lied to you about the shopping trip. I didn't mean to hurt you."

"Why didn't you want me to come shopping with me?"

"It wasn't like that! Amber offered to come with me and had already invited Sarah along."

"So you *are* embarrassed to be seen with me!"

"No!" I lie. "I just didn't think they would be your type... that's all!"

"They look a bit up 'emselves, if you ask me." she sniffs.

"They're okay...when you get to know them," I reply. "Are we still friends then?"

"I s'pose so," she sighs. "Do you wanna hear the new Killers CD?"

"Yeah, Okay." I smile as I put Missie down and sit on the bed.

17:00

"I'll see you in December...I promise!" Brian wipes a tear from OB's cheek as they stand at the door.

"Oh pleeeease! Get a room!" I say, as he snogs her face off! "Oh no, sorry! You can't can you...he's got to go back to the ship!"

"Bye, kiddo!" he ruffles my hair as he speaks. Grrrrrrrrrr! Why do adults think it's okay to do that? "I'll miss you!"

"Whatever!"

17:05

Hooray! He's gone! Back to being just me and Mum!

CHAPTER FOUR
Peer Pressure

Thursday 1 November

OB has been a complete nightmare since Brian left. She's turned into some sort of personal jailer! I know she misses him, but there's no need to take it out on me!

07:45

"Oh good, you're ready for school. You can tidy your room before you go then!"

Duh! Total waste of time! What's the point of tidying my room? – It'll just get messy again in a couple of days, so I might as well just leave it as it is!

08:15

Total humiliation! Not only did she insist on walking me to school (something she's not done since I was about seven) she's just hugged me and given me a kiss outside the school gate!

If anyone who knows me saw that, my life is ruined! I will deny knowing her and tell them that she was some nutter who just came up to me and hugged me.

"Take care when you come home. Remember to cross the road carefully!"

She's been like this for days! She's been setting all sorts of stupid rules.

"Come back by five o'clock."

"Don't walk to Amber's on your own."

"Make sure you stick to large crowds."

And the best one,

"Don't go on the top floor of a double-decker bus!"

What is going on? She's acting like I'm three years old again. It's complete madness!! I swear if she doesn't give me back my independence, she'll be sorry if I have to take a stand and rebel.

17:00

"So, have you got any homework on?"

Grrrrr. She's really getting on my nerves now! This question is always followed by a lecture on homework – as is "So, what book are you reading in class?" This always leads to an argument about homework - which normally leads into argument about just about everything that I've ever done wrong in my life and ends with her saying "because I said so," – which isn't really a reason at all but she seems to think that it is! As if the constant reminders of her expectations for me to succeed in my exams aren't enough – why can't she just LEAVE ME ALONE!

21:00

I have come to the conclusion that I must be adopted. I can't possibly have been produced by this mad woman! I can't wait 'til I leave home. I'll get a job as a solicitor, like Dad, and get loads of money. We'll see who's laughing when I sue her for mental cruelty! Ha! Ha!

Friday 2 November

Why, why, why does no-one fancy me? Must be the moosiest moose in the school as I seem to be the only one without a boyfriend!

12:30

I listen to the rain hammering against the window as I eat my lettuce and cucumber salad. Mmm tasty! I've taken to eating my lunch in the library on my own. I can hide at one of the small tables behind the shelves of books so no-one can see me eating. Anyway, it's better than having to watch everybody else eating whatever they want. I'm determined that this diet is going to work.

12:32

I finish my lunch and decide to move to one of the seats in the open library. I like it here. It's nice to have a place to come where you can just sit and enjoy the peace. I can see the other students as they pass by the library through the row of windows.

I watch my friends giggle with their boyfriends as they walk in the direction of the school canteen for lunch – well, I presume that's where they are heading to, as it's so wet outside. Everyone seems to have a girlfriend or boyfriend – apart from me that is! Even Fat Fiona (a greasy haired lump of lard from Class 5c) has got a boyfriend!! Granted it is Geeky Geoff, a four foot seven weed with buck teeth, acne and lego hair who wears bottle end glasses! – and even *they* managed to pull!! I must be soooo ugly!!!!!

12:45

I remember that I promised Amber that I would meet her in the canteen. I grab a bottle of water from the vending machine and quickly head there. I reach the canteen and spot Amber,

Sarah and India sat at one of the tables in the far corner of the room. They have their heads together and are obviously in deep conversation.

"Hadn't you heard? India says, pausing for dramatic effect.

The others shake their heads as they stare at her, waiting for the conclusion of what she is about to announce. She is obviously enjoying the fact that she knows something that they don't and smirks as I approach the table.

"Oh Hi, Anne! She greets me, milking the fact that she knows she is keeping them waiting for their piece of juicy gossip.

"Never mind that! Sit down, Anne!" barks Sarah, almost drooling with excitement. "India, will you just tell us what's happened to Abi!"

"She's only gone and got herself...pregnant!" India is delighted to be the bearer of such a major newsflash! "Her mum and dad have removed her from the school!"

"But that's awful!" I cry. "Surely she should be with her friends at a time like this. She shouldn't have to be on her own."

"What does Gareth think about it?" asked Amber.

"He's dumped her!" India replied, loving being the centre of attention.

"What, Liam's friend Gareth?" I ask.

"The very same!" India nodded.

"I've got no sympathy!" Sarah scoffs. "She should have been more careful...I always am with Jack!"

"I know, I always insist on using protection!" agreed Amber.

What? They're actually having sex with their boyfriends? I can't believe that my friends are actually DOING it!

"I even make them use a flavoured one if they want a BJ!" laughs India. "Well, it's better to be safe than sorry!"

"That's nothing! Anna tells me she wears rubber gloves just to give a boy a handshake!" Amber sniggers.

Oh that's right, make me the butt of your jokes AGAIN! I feel myself going bright red as they scream with laughter. I start to panic. I must be the only virgin left in the school!

From what they were saying in sex education, the thought of doing it with a boy sounds totally gross! To be honest, I don't feel anywhere near ready to go all the way – I mean, I've only just had my first proper snog! I'm too embarrassed to admit to my friends that I haven't got a clue what they are on about most of the time.

"No I don't!" I reply indignantly. "I've held hands with boys a lot and I don't wear gloves!"

There that told them! Hang on a minute…why are they all falling about laughing?

Saturday 3 November

I've seen three girls already at school copying my haircut and colour. I never knew that Ronald McDonald would turn out to be a style icon! Maybe that's why Sarah, India and Amber have asked me to go shopping with them today?

13:00

"Right, we'd better get back to the shops!" Sarah barks as we finish our lunch.

"Can't we just have five more minutes? My feet are killing me!" India complains, stretching her feet under the table.

Fine by me, I think as I sip my coffee. We've been shopping all morning as it is. I don't really need to buy anything and have just come out for the trip. My feet are aching too so I'm quite happy sitting here in the warm of Lorenzo's Italian Coffee Shop, with the smell of freshly ground coffee filling my nostrils – I love that smell!

"Okay, but just five minutes! We've got things to do this afternoon!" Sarah orders.

It's really cold outside today. Although it's not raining, the sky is charcoal grey. The lack of sunshine makes the dark wood in the coffee shop look even darker than usual, but the happy chatter of the customers and the heat from the ovens and coffee machines makes the place feel much brighter than it actually is. As I enjoy the cosy atmosphere, I can feel my enthusiasm for the shopping trip draining quicker than my coffee cup.

14:00

Primark? Now *this* is somewhere I didn't expect Sarah to want to shop!" I think to myself as she drags us into the low budget clothes store.

"Sarah, why have we come to Chavsville?" asks Amber.

"You're not actually going to buy something from *here* are you?" India turns up her nose.

"As if!" Sarah splutters. "No, I thought this would be the perfect place for Anne to have her initiation!"

"What initiation?" I ask, suddenly feeling nervous as I look at Amber and India's worried faces.

"You're going to find me a top to wear tonight...and none of us are going to pay for it!" Sarah smiles.

"What?...You mean steal it?"

"It's only worthless junk anyway...You'll be doing the rest of Brighton a favour by saving them from having to buy it!"

"But...I've never..."

"Do you want to be part of this group or not?" she sneers.

"Well...yes...but..."

"So what are you waiting for?" she raises her eyes. "Come with me!"

I obediently follow her as she grabs a couple of tops and marches into the changing room. She beckons for me to follow her into a cubicle. I follow her behind the curtain and she hangs the clothes on a hook on the wall. She plunges her hand into her bag and starts to rummage inside.

"Ah! Here they are! She says triumphantly as she pulls out a pair of scissors. "Once you've picked out a decent top for me, you need to bring it in here. Make sure you bring some others with you though! Then you can prise the tag off and put it in your bag."

"I don't know about this!" I am feeling very uneasy. I've never done anything like this before and I'm not sure I want to start!

"It's easy...Look I'll show you!" Sarah expertly prises the tag off the top. "Then all that's left is to put it in your bag and take the other garments back!"

"Isn't there something else I could do instead?" I ask hopefully.

"Not if you want to prove yourself as a friend worth having!" she replies. "We'll meet you outside when you've done it."

Sarah leaves me in the cubicle with the tops she has discarded. I feel sick. I remove the two tops from the hook and take them back onto the shop floor. Maybe Amber can persuade her to give me something else to do.

14:02

They've gone! I look around the shop and can't see any sign of my friends. What am I going to do? If I do it, I might get caught – but if I don't do it, Sarah will never speak to me again!

14:03

I can see them outside. They must be waiting for me. I feel guilty already as I look around the shop to try and find something that Sarah might approve of. Ugh, tat – all of it!

14:04

Wait a minute! That one looks alright. I begin to tremble as I walk towards the display of sparkly t-shirts. I pick three t-shirts from the rail and walk back to the changing rooms, armed with the pair of scissors. I can't believe I'm actually doing this!

14:05

It's off! I got the tag off! I feel like I'm going to faint as I shove the t-shirt into my bag and walk out of the changing rooms. I start to sweat as I place the other t-shirts back onto the rail and hurry out of the shop.

14:06

Oh my God! I've done it! I give the girls a thumbs up sign as I walk towards them. I just want to give the t-shirt to Sarah as quickly as possible and forget all about it. I wonder if it's really theft if you're not nicking something for yourself?

14:07

"Excuse me, Miss?" Would you be kind enough to accompany me back to the store? I've reason to believe that you may have something in your possession that you haven't paid for."

I freeze in panic as I feel the security guard grab my arm. As I turn to face him, my friends scarper. Suddenly, I really need a pee! The security guard is huge – he's holding my arm tightly as he takes me back into the shop. I'm so scared! What's going to happen to me? Will they ring the police? Will they ring Mum? OB is going to kill me!

17:00

That was a nightmare! The security guard was fierce (I swear some of these people get a kick out of making people scared) but the Store Manager was really nice. He was about the same age as my dad and, after making me sweat for nearly three hours, he must have taken pity on me because he's let me off with a caution – and a ban from the shop (as if I'm ever likely to step foot in here again anyway!).

However, it's not over yet. OB is sitting outside and they are just about to let me go – so I've got to face her now!

21:00

I don't know what was worse – the fear of her anger – or the look of sheer disappointment on her face as they led me out of the Store Manager's office. We travelled home in silence. I guess she was too shocked to be angry with me – I suppose that will come later. She offered me some dinner - but I felt too sick with shame to eat, so I came straight upstairs to my room.

Monday 5 November

Normally I love fireworks night – but this year, I'm doing my best to avoid them!

12:30

"Thanks a bunch for running off like that!" I glare at my friends as I walk up to their table at lunchtime.

"Well it's not our fault you got caught!" sniffs Sarah.

"You can't expect us to get into trouble just because you mess up!" agrees India.

"At least she tried." Amber adds, kindly.

"I s'pose!" Sarah nods. "At least I've still got the top that I took when I was showing her how to do it!"

"I never want to go through anything like that again!" I laugh, relieved to be forgiven.

"Technically, you failed the task. I should really think of something else for you to do." Sarah gives me a wicked grin.

"Don't be mean!" Amber cries. "She's been through enough…and she *did* keep us all out of it, so that should prove something!"

"Well, it's lucky for you that I'm such a soft touch, isn't it, Anne? Consider your initiation over!"

17:00

I can hear fireworks outside! I rush over to my bedroom window to watch them. Great it's dark already! Fireworks always look so much better in the dark! I've loved fireworks ever since I can remember. When I was little, I used to be scared of the bangs. The really loud ones still make me jump but I watch excitedly as air-bombs and rockets fill the sky with colourful stars. It's so beautiful!

17:15

"I thought you might like some hot chocolate to go with those fireworks!" OB says as she comes into my bedroom with two cups of steaming cocoa.

"Thanks, Mum" I smile at her as I take the mug she is holding out to me.

Hot chocolate is the drink we always have on Fireworks night – it's a sort of tradition. Normally we have it because we watch outside in the cold – but it's nice being here, just me and Mum, watching out of the window. Somehow this symbol of peace gives me the same warm feeling inside.

Saturday 10 November

I have foolishly agreed to baby-sit for the brats again this afternoon. At least Steph is coming with me so it shouldn't be too bad!

11:00

"Body armour."

"Check!"

"Ear Defenders."

"Check!"

"First Aid Kit"

"Check!"

"Numbers for all emergency services!"

"Check"

"Right I think we're about ready to baby-sit your dad's little angels then!"

Steph and me giggle as we walk downstairs to the car, where OB is waiting to take us to dad's house.

11:30

"Now you girls know where everything is don't you! Mummy just wants to say bye-bye to my wittle sweethearts!" Belinda leaves to fetch the brats.

I giggle as Steph mimes putting two fingers down her throat to be sick!

Belinda enters the room in a cloud of Calvin Klein and hands Josh to me and bends down to give Brat Number One a kiss.

"Bye- Bye, Olivia. Mummy's going out for a while now. You be a good little girl for your sister and her nice friend Stephanie."

"Fat chance!" I whisper to Steph. And she's *not* my sister!

Josh decides he doesn't want to be held by me and smashes me over the head with his toy train to make sure I let go of him.

"Ow!" I yell. "That hurt you little…"

I let Devil's Spawn go and all hell breaks loose.

"Waaaaaaaaaah" wails brat Number One.

Oh that's right, we can't have anyone having the attention now can we Olivia!

"Look what you've done now! You've frightened her!" yells Belinda as she rushes to pick Olivia up.

Josh hits me on the head again with a particularly vicious blow and I yelp in pain.

"David! Will you come and sort your children out - Please!" Belinda bellows.

"Oh My God! Your head's bleeding!" screeches Steph.

"Waaaaaaah" wails Brat Number One

"What the hell's going on?" roars dad as he runs into the room.

"Oooooooh it really hurts!" I cry

"There, there baby! It's alright," Belinda soothes Brat Number One who continues to bawl.

"Josh! Will you come back here!" shouts Dad as Devil's Spawn runs from the room, yelling and waving his train above his head like a trophy.

"WILL SOMEBODY PLEASE HELP ME - I THINK HE'S FRACTURED MY SKULL!!

15:00

After almost four hours of waiting in the Accident and Emergency Department of the Royal Sussex County Hospital, I leave with half a dozen stitches in my head. Belinda has been giving me the evils since we got here. She seems to blame me for missing out on her shopping trip.

"I'll take you girls home," offers Dad.

"But we can still make the shops if we try!" Belinda whines.

"Forget the shops, Belinda." he grunts.

"It's okay, Dad. I'll phone Mum."

"I'm not leaving you until I know you're home safely!" he insists.

"I just thought that if we could make the last hour…"

"Belinda! My daughter has just come out of hospital…the shops can wait!" he loosens the neck of his shirt, like he always does when he's getting angry.

"Oh that's right! Let her ruin the rest of the day!" she huffs.

"WILL YOU SHUT UP ABOUT THE BLOODY SHOPS!"

Hilarious! She couldn't have looked more shocked if he'd slapped her across the face!

17:00

Am now taking bets against Dad and Belinda actually making their wedding!

Tuesday 13 November

I can't believe I was actually put in hospital by a three year old! I've told everyone at school that I hit my head after falling over drunk – they were well impressed!

17:30

"Hello, Darling"

"Oh, Hi Dad!"

"Just phoning to see how you're feeling. How's the head?"

"Better than it was!"

"Belinda feels terrible about what happened."

"Really!" I reply in my best sarcastic tone.

"She's bought you a big box of chocolates to apologize."

"Oh great!" I mutter under my breath.

"You don't sound too thrilled?"

"Duh! I'm on a diet! I don't *do* chocolate!"

"I see…er, well…I'm sure we can get you something else instead."

"No, please …don't bother!"

"Must go! Belinda's just put my dinner on the table. Look after yourself."

Sure! Bye, Dad!"

18:00

My head is actually feeling quite painful at the moment. I think I *will* treat myself to some chocolate after all.

18:01

Yes! I've found a Mars Bar left over from my emergency stash in my wardrobe. My emergency stash has always been kept there for times of pain and misery (physical or mental). I think *now* qualifies as such a time. Come to Mama! Mmmmmmm!

18:10

Major guilt trip about breaking diet with Mars Bar. Managed to throw it up again so I hope the calories don't count! It seems such a waste - Oh well, it was nice while it lasted!

Friday 16 November

I've been invited to a sleepover for Amber's birthday tomorrow. Can't wait!!

11:00

It's so nice to have Tom back teaching us English. Listening to his voice makes me drool, which can be a problem sometimes as I forget to concentrate on what he's actually saying!

11:05

I love the way the back of his hair curls over the neck of his jacket when he turns round to write on the white board.

11:10

He looks tired. Probably due to sleepless nights with baby. I bet he's the type that insists on doing his share of the night feeds!

Or, maybe he's had a row with his wife? She's probably suffering from chronic post-natal depression and he's having to do everything while he's at home. Look after the baby, cook, clean the house, get up in the night AND come to work and mark our homework – He's such a hero!

Yes, that's probably it! He'll be so fed up with her selfishness that he'll end up looking for comfort elsewhere. Can I help it if I just happen to be the one he turns to in his hour of need?

11:30

I must stop having fantasies about my married English teacher. I am a strong independent woman and don't need a man in my life to make it complete. I'm quite happy enjoying time with my friends thank you very much!

11:31

He *has* got a lovely voice though! (sigh!)

13:00

"As my Bitch Mother From Hell won't let me have a party for my birthday, I've decided what I want to do!" Amber announces to Sarah, India and me as we walk back to class after lunch-break.

"I love birthdays! What are we doing then?" India replies.

"A sleepover! We can watch a DVD and have pizza and do makeovers and stuff – it'll be cool! I'm only inviting you three though 'cos there's only room for three mattresses in my bedroom!"

"Why don't we make a day of it? We can go shopping in the morning and then all go back to your house for the sleepover later!" suggests Sarah.

"I'm not sure I'm ready for another one of your shopping trips!" I reply nervously.

"It's okay, I promise there'll be no freebies this time!" Sarah laughs.

"That's settled then! We'll all meet round my house at eleven. Bring your sleeping bags or duvets with you - you can dump them in my bedroom before we go."

Cool! My first ever sleepover!

Steph and me have been on the phone for an hour, talking about – well not much really. I look at the clock and see that it is nearly nine o'clock.

"We'd better get of the phone...Ugly Betty's on in a minute!" Not that I should need to remind her as neither of us have missed an episode – it's soooo funny!

"Excellent! I'll see you tomorrow then. I'm really looking forward to it, aren't you?"

OMG! I have completely forgotten that I'd promised Steph I'd go to the cinema with her tomorrow night to see the sing-along version of the Sound of Music. (her choice not mine!)

"Er...I'm really sorry Steph...I've, sort of promised Amber I'd go round to hers for a sleepover." I cringe.

"I see!" Oh no, I can tell she's hurt.

"I'm sorry...it's her birthday and I promised I'd go. I completely forgot about the film!"

Silence - I panic. What can I do to make it up for her. Brilliant idea – I am a total genius!

"We can always go to see the film on Sunday!" I suggest, feeling smug with myself for being such a brilliant problem solver.

"I'll tell you what Anne, let's not bother!" she replied. "I'm sick of always being second best. You go and enjoy your sleepover...I'll go to the cinema with someone who *wants* my company!"

"But, Steph!"

"Goodbye, Anne…have a nice life!"

What? She's actually hung up on me! She probably thinks I'm going to ring back and beg her to go and see a stupid film that I didn't even want to go and see in the first place – As if!

Saturday 17 November

Amber's sleepover – Must remember to take duvet and pillow. I've packed my favourite PJs and a wash bag and towel. I've no idea what else to take. What do people do at a sleepover anyway?

11:30

With our duvets safely stored in Amber's bedroom, the four of us walked to the bus-stop to wait for the bus to take us into Brighton shopping centre.

"It's only a few stops. We really should walk...you know, saving the environment and all that!" I suggest.

"Duh! If we walk, we'll wear out our shoes and have to buy new ones, which have probably been made in some sweat shop in India. I think we owe it to those poor people who work in such appalling conditions to keep our shoe purchases to a minimum." Sarah snorts. "Unless, you see a pair that you simply must have to go with the new outfit you've just bought ...then you just *have* to buy them."

13:00

Amber is certainly making the most of the opportunity to spend her birthday money. It's a bit boring trekking round Brighton shopping when everyone else has the money to spend. I've only got my £50 pocket money – and that's got to last me for the whole week!

"I'm starving!" cries Amber. "Birthday chocolate cake at Lorenzo's everyone?"

"Yum, their chocolate fudge cake is to die for!" agrees India.

We take our place in the queue at Lorenzo's. The counter has the biggest display of gateaux in the area. They are all hand made by Lorenzo and scream "eat me!" positively defying you to you walk by without choosing one. Amber, India and Sarah all choose their favourites and their eyes bulge with lust as the huge slices are handed over the counter to them. I am completely saintly as I resist temptation and order a small skinny latte. We pay at the till at the end of the counter and find a spare table.

"Aren't you having any cake, Anne?" asks Amber as she notices my tray only carries a coffee.

"I can't, I'm on a diet." I mumble.

"What do *you* need to diet for? You're the thinnest of all of us!" she laughs.

"Yeah, right!" I reply.

"Yeah, you even make Keira Knightly look fat!" laughs Sarah.

I scowl at them. They're supposed to be my friends and yet I'm always the butt of their jokes. It's not fair! They won't be laughing when I really *am* slim – I'll show them then!

14:00

Suddenly realise that I haven't bought Amber a present. I didn't actually know it was her birthday until yesterday so I've not had a chance to get her anything. I feel really bad.

14:01

I have a brilliant idea!

140

"Amber, I haven't had a chance to buy you a present. How about you choose something while we're out?"

"Really? You mean clothes?" she asks excitedly.

"Yes, maybe a new top or something." I reply, imagining a cool new t-shirt or similar.

"Brilliant! There's a top I've been wanting for ages...I'll show you!"

Amber drags us all into River Island and heads straight for the jumpers. She plucks a long grey and black striped jumper from the rail and holds it up in front of her.

"Isn't it gorgeous!" she squeals.

I gulp as I see the price tag. Thirty-five pounds! I hadn't intended to spend that much.

"Are you sure that's the one you want?" I frantically look around to see if I can spot anything cool in the T-Shirt section. Excellent! There's one that Gwen Stefani herself would be proud to wear.

"Ooooooh look at that T-Shirt, Amber! That would look so cool on you!" I point out the fab T-Shirt, hoping that she'll like that better (well at least it's only £19.99!)

Amber looks so disappointed I immediately feel really mean. She'd set her heart on the jumper – and I have to admit, it *is* really gorgeous.

"No? Okay, the jumper it is!" I shrug.

"Thank you, Anne! You're the best!" she cries as she twirls around the shop floor to make sure that everyone can see her new jumper.

141

I just hope she appreciates that I'm going to have to live on fifteen pounds for the rest of the week!

20:00

"Do you want this last piece of pizza?" India asks me, whilst she looks at the remaining slice longingly.

"No thanks. I've had too much already," I reply.

"That's funny…I haven't seen you have any?" Sarah looks puzzled.

"Duh! I've had three slices!...I probably just ate them so fast you didn't see me" I lied. "I'm such a pig when it comes to pizza!"

"Oh well, if no-one else wants it!" India licks her lips as she helps herself to the last of the food.

"Right! Who's for a makeover?" I can't believe my eyes when Amber unveils a tray, overflowing with bottles and tubes. My make-up collection looks meagre beside it. I've no idea what half of it is and I stare with amazement at the selection of vicious looking instruments that look as though they would be equally at home on a surgeon's trolley.

20:01

"Ow! That hurts! I cry.

"Stop wriggling will you or you'll end up with wonky eyebrows!" Amber replies as she waves a pair of tweezers in front of my eye.

"I'll probably end up with no eyebrows at all if your hair-dying skills are anything to go by!" I wince as she tears another tweezer full of hair from my forehead.

"You are not in a position to get funny with me, Madam!" she laughs. "Right, now for the face pack!"

20:20

"I cant nove ny hace!" The face pack has dried hard on my face and is pulling my skin.

"It must be dry!" India laughs. "She says she can't move her face!"

Amber drags me into the bathroom to wash off the mask. It's a relief to get the horrible stuff off my face. Once all the mask is off she drags me back into the bedroom. I look in the mirror and wonder why women would actually pay to have their face look red and blotchy like this.

"Don't worry, we'll cover that with make-up," Amber explains confidently.

For over half an hour, I have Amber applying make-up to my face, India doing something to my hair with curling tongs and Sarah busily painting my nails with a French manicure.

21:00

At last they've finished!

"Wow! You look really pretty!" Amber says as she stands back to admire her handy work.

Finally, they let me look in the mirror to see what they've done to me and – OMG! I look like some sort of freaked-out poodle!

23:30

After three more make-overs, (who said you can't have too much of a good thing!) we all take our make-up off and get ready for bed. I can't help but wonder what the point of it all was as I go to the bathroom to get changed into my night clothes.

23:35

I return to the bedroom dressed in my pink "princess" pyjamas and freeze as I see the other girls are all wearing vests and boxer shorts. I feel like such a child! I just want the ground to open up and swallow me. I don't think I'm cut out for this sleepover stuff!

Saturday 24 November

What is wrong with everybody this week? Everyone seems to be on my back!

08:00

Whoever invented the alarm clock should be shot! I've had a bad week and just want to roll up inside my duvet and go back to sleep. My so called friends haven't stopped going on about my pyjamas and have been calling me "Princess" all week. Okay, so maybe they're not exactly cool, but I really wish they'd drop the subject.

Steph hasn't been in touch all week – and hasn't even returned my text messages. Well I've apologized three times. I'm not trying any more.

OB's even started nagging again. She keeps trying to force food down me because she's got it into her head that I've got Anorexia! Duh! How stupid is that? I'm even beginning to wish Brian was back – at least she'd butt out of my business then!

09:00

"Good afternoon!"

"Very funny, Mum. If you're going to start nagging me again, I'm going back to bed!"

"Oh dear, someone *has* got out of the wrong side of the bed this morning."

"My bed's by the wall. I got out the same side as I always do!"

"Here, eat this toast," she shoves a plate of toast in front of me. "Maybe that'll put you in a better mood."

"I'm not hungry!" I push the toast away.

"This diet is going too far, Anne! Just eat the toast," she sighs as she pushes the plate back in front of me.

To my surprise, she sits at the table opposite to watch me eat it. I pick up a half-slice and start to nibble on it, to please her. I try to give her my "I was going to eat it anyway so don't think you sitting there watching me is going to make any difference" look but she's not looking at me any more. She's sat with her head in her hands. Why is she crying? It's only a piece of toast!

13:00

I hear the postman pushing something through our letter-box. I run to fetch the mail for mum. Maybe there'll be a letter from Brian to cheer her up (she's been in a weird mood all morning!). I think she must be upset that he hasn't been in touch again since he left. She keeps making excuses for him, saying that he's too busy to contact her, but I know she's upset really.
Oh good! A postcard! I wonder who it's from? It's from Israel – must be from Mags! Oh well, it's not Brian but it should at least cheer her up a bit.

"Here you are Mum," I say as I hand OB the pile of post. "There's a postcard from Mags in there."

Her face brightens as she begins to read the postcard out loud.

Shalom!

I bet you're impressed! Four weeks in Israel and I'm speaking fluent Hebrew already!

Life in the Kibbutz is harder than I expected. We have to work seven hours a day in the fields in return for free accommodation. I suppose they do feed us for that as well. (And no getting any ideas about using me as slave labour when I get home Mum!)

I share a room (well more of a cupboard really) with Maddie and Sian. It's just as well we've become really good friends because it's a bit on the cosy side in there.

I've decided to continue travelling with the girls. We will be moving on from here in four weeks – before we collapse with exhaustion. I've no idea where we'll be heading, but I'll let you know when we've made our minds up!

Love to you all.

Mags

"I really miss her," OB sniffs as she finishes reading.

"Yeah, me too, Mum."

Tuesday 27 November

I've got nothing to do today - half term is boring without Steph!

10:30

"Hi, Anne," Amber is stood on my doorstep. "India and I are just going to the Meeting Place. Do you fancy coming?"

Ha! Steph, I've got other friends to hang out with!

"I'll just get my coat!" I reply and grab my coat from the hook in the hallway.

The weather has turned freezing cold. The rain turns into sleet as we turn onto the seafront and the icy particles burn my cheeks as we walk to the café. I pull the collar of my coat up around my face to try and protect myself from the wind. The sea sounds like thunder as it throws the waves up onto the pebbles on the beach below us.

"Hey, watch this!" India shouts as she blows into the cold air, her breath leaving a trail in her path, giving the impression that she's smoking a cigarette.

We all giggle as we walk along the seafront, pretending to be smoking. We must look sooooo cool.

11:45

We are all shivering as we reach the café. I feel so cold that I decide to allow myself a milky coffee to warm my body. We choose a table in the corner and sit down to drink our coffee, still wrapped up in our coats. I'm not so sure that an open air café was such a good idea today!

"I think we should find somewhere a bit warmer to hang out." I shiver.

"We can all go round to mine and watch a DVD if you like," suggests Amber.

"As long as Anne doesn't do any more rubbish impressions!" Sarah laughs.

"Ha! Ha! Very funny," I reply as I finish my coffee.

"That's the problem…They're not!" Sarah laughs as Amber and India join in.

"I see! I'm butt of the joke again…what a novelty!"

12:00

"Hey, isn't that Tom?" asks Amber as she looks across at a table at the far end of the café.

"Where?" I try to spot him but she is blocking my view.

"Over there!" she points. "I wonder who the elephant is with him?"

We stand up to join Sarah and India, who have already stood up and are tying their scarves around their necks. I move to the side to try and see where she's pointing. It *is* him! I can see him sitting at a table bouncing a baby boy on his knee. He looks really happy as he laughs at something someone sat opposite has just said to him. I look across the table to see a huge woman. Amber wasn't joking when she said elephant!
We make our way out of the restaurant but our path takes us straight past his table.

"Hello girls!" he smiles, when he spots us.

150

"Hi, Tom" (or similar) we all reply.

"I'd like you to meet my son, William," he looks really proud as he introduces the plump little baby.

William looks so cute with his blonde hair just visible under his bobble hat that we can't resist crowding round for a better look.

"This," he says equally proudly, "Is my wife, Stacey."

His wife! I can't believe that someone as fit as him could be married to someone like her, let alone be proud of her. I mean, apart from being ENORMOUS, she's old – she must be at least twenty six or something!
    I wonder if the others are as shocked as me as we walk to Amber's house? We're going to watch Shallow Hal. I'm not sure what that's about.

18:00

Elizabeth runs into the living room followed by her drippy husband, Nathan. He's carrying Lilly, who giggles as he bounces her up and down in his arms.

"Hi Sis," Elizabeth gives me a big hug and then pulls away with a worried look on her face. "What are you doing to yourself? I can feel your ribs through that jumper!"

"You tell her Elizabeth!" OB starts. "I've been trying to tell her she's taking that diet too far but will she listen to me? No she won't! You talk to her Elizabeth because she won't listen to me!"

"Well never mind, fat or thin, you'll always be ugly! Ain't that right kid?" laughs Nathan.

I run from the room in tears. I'm a no-hoper if even Nathan thinks I'm ugly!!

"Thanks a bunch, you idiot!" I hear Elizabeth say as I leave the room.

"What? What did I say?" Nathan replies as I shut and lock my bedroom door.

19:00

"Hey, Sis! Let me in will you?" Elizabeth knocks my door.

"Go away!" I sulk.

"Come on Anne, I want to talk to you," she pleads.

I drag myself off my bed and walk across my room to open the door. Elizabeth smiles at me as she walks in.

"Thanks," she looks at me with the same look OB always gives me when she's about to lecture me. "I'm sorry about Nathan earlier. You don't want to take any notice of anything he says. He's a complete idiot!"

"Duh! Tell me something I don't already know!"

"Mums right though, Sis. You *are* losing a lot of weight. Are you okay?"

"Don't *you* start. I've got enough with mum going on at me. She's convinced herself that I've got anorexia...she's doing my head in!" I laugh - but she doesn't laugh with me.

"Look me in the eye and tell me you're not anorexic!" she stares into my eyes waiting for me to answer her.

"I – am – on – a – diet!" I reply. "That doesn't make me anorexic!"

"Okay, have it your own way. But I'm here if you need me," she sighs as she gets up from my bed and walks out of my room.

Anorexic! That's really funny! Right?

CHAPTER FIVE
Xmas is for Children

Saturday 1 December

Xmas will be here soon. I have decided that I want to be more sophisticated this year. Instead of lots of small presents in a pillowcase, I want one special present under the tree.

08:00

"You're going to have to tell me what you want for Christmas this year or I'm not going to have long for Christmas Shopping." OB says as she butters a slice of toast.

"You won't need long for my present this year," I smile. "I've decided that all that presents in a pillowcase at the bedroom door stuff is for kids. This year, I'd like just one really good present under the tree."

"Well, if you're sure?" she sounds doubtful.

"Yup, I'm too old for all that rubbish now." I nod.

"Okay, if that's what you want," she shrugs. "But you'll still have to let me know what you want."

"That's easy, I'd love an MP4!" I say hopefully.

"I bet you would," she replies.

"Too expensive?"

"Maybe a bit. You'll just have to wait and see," she smiles.

Yes! I knew she'd buy me one!

10:00

I've decided that I'd better make a start on my Christmas card list. If I want to get loads of cards this year, I'd better give mine out early so they won't forget to send me one back!

OB	Abi
Dad	Liam
Belinda	Gareth
Josh	Jack
Olivia	Samantha
Elizabeth	Bethany
Nathan	Sophie
Lilly	Karyn
Mags	Toby
Steph	Jon
Amber	Joseph
Sarah	Kayleigh
India	Tom

Total cards needed = 26. Better buy a pack of 30 just in case anyone does send me a card that I forgot.

10:30

What am I doing? What happened to the grown up Christmas? Will not be vain and send cards to people I don't like just to get more cards back. Will cut down the list to those people I really want to send cards to.

OB	Abi
Dad	~~Liam~~ (He's a pig!)
~~Belinda~~ (she can go on Dad's card)	~~Gareth~~ (So is he)
~~Josh~~ (so can he)	~~Jack~~ (So is he)
~~Olivia~~ (so can she)	Samantha
Elizabeth	Bethany
~~Nathan~~ (he can go on Sis' card)	~~Sophie~~ (she's stuck up)
~~Lilly~~ (so can she)	Karyn

158

Mags (would send but no address!) Toby
Steph (she's not speaking to me!) Jon
Amber Joseph
Sarah Kayleigh
India Tom (better add William)
(and Stacey I suppose!)

Total cards needed = 15. Will buy 20 – just in case!!

Sunday 2 December

It's Devil's Spawn's birthday today! Dad and Belinda asked me to go over and help with the games at his party. This year, I'm not bothering to dress up. It was days before I finally stopped finding food in the pockets of my clothes after last year's party. By the time I had spotted the remains of jelly and ice-cream in the inside pocket of my coat, it was ruined. This year, I'm going after they've finished eating!

14:00

"Oh good you're here!" Dad looks relived. "We're just about to open his presents...it's getting a bit chaotic in there!"

"Looks like I'm just in time then," I smile, holding up my carefully wrapped gift.

We walk back into the living room where the brats and their friends were settling down for Josh to open his presents. Dad takes my parcel and places it with the huge, colourful pile of objects that his friends had brought with them. Belinda sits Josh on her knee so she can open the presents for him as Dad hands them to her.

I sit and watch as toy after toy is unwrapped and can only imagine the hours of pain they are going to cause! At last! They've got to my present. He's going to love this. It's vile (like him!) but at least it's soft – a brilliant match!

Belinda peels open the sparkly blue paper that I chose. And unwraps the soft furry toy. I can see the big black furry body as she lifts it out of the paper.

"Ugh! A spider!...it's horrible!" Belinda squeals.

Devil's Spawn, of course, loves it and grabs the gigantic fluffy tarantula and proceeds to terrorise all his friends with it. The place is turned into chaos within seconds. It's hilarious! Children scream as Josh charges after them with the spider and

161

Belinda tries to comfort some of the traumatised kids while Dad manages to catch Josh and take his prized toy away from him.

It seems that most of the kids aren't in the mood for a party any more and the mums that are already here take their over-sensitive little darlings with them. Belinda sits with her arm round Brat Number One as she telephones the remaining children's mums to collect them. Dad attempts to settle the others by doing an impromptu puppet show from behind the sofa. (I used to love it when he did that when I was younger!)

14:30

At last! They've all gone!

"You stupid girl!" Belinda snapped as she closed the door to the last of the mothers.

"I'm sorry," I apologize, trying my best to sound sincere. "I didn't realize he'd go mad like that. Still, at least he liked his present!"

Now, what can I get him for Christmas?

Tuesday 4 December

OB is over the moon! Brian is coming back. Oh, joy!

13:00

Yawn! Are boys *all* they can talk about? Okay, I'll admit to being a little bit jealous that they've all got boyfriends but it does get boring! They're all talking about the Christmas Party. Sarah's going with Jack, India's going with Toby and Amber with Joseph. Me? I guess I'll be going on my own (as usual!). Steph and me used to talk about all sorts of things.

"Has anyone seen Abi lately?" I ask, to change the subject.

"I went round at the weekend. She's getting really bored at home," replies Amber.

"At least she doesn't have to come to school," India laughs.

"Her mum and dad are paying for a private tutor. She reckons its way more boring than school," Amber leans in towards the rest of us to avoid the other tables in the canteen overhearing our conversation.

"She must be getting pretty fat by now," Sarah turns her nose up as she speaks.

"Enormous!" Amber nods. "And the baby's not due until March!"

"Ugh! I'm never having a baby! I couldn't stand having to wear all those horrible clothes!" Sarah shudders at the thought.

"No way!" agree the others.

19:30

OB's mobile goes off just as the theme for Eastenders starts to play on the TV.

"Damn! I wanted to see if Dawn was going to choose Jase or Gary," she moans as she picks up the phone.

She flips open the phone and reads the screen. She squeals with excitement when she sees who the message is from.

"It's from Brian!" she gasps.

I can't believe my eyes. She says she's over him – and yet the first time he bothers to contact her since he left the house she can hardly hold the phone, her hands are trembling that much as she presses the button to read the message. I just don't get it!

"He's coming home! – Tomorrow!" she cries as she reads his message.

Oh great!

Suddenly all thoughts about Dawn, Gary and Jase seem to have left her head as she spends the rest of the evening texting Brian and waiting for his replies. Honestly, it's worse than being with my mates!

Wednesday 5 December

B-Day – Brian lands at Gatwick!

07:00

"Wake up Anne! You haven't got time to stay in bed all morning. You need to tidy your room before you go to school. I want the house to look nice for when Brian gets here!"

Oh God! She's going to be a nightmare!

"Mum, why do I have to tidy my room? He's not ever going to see it!"

"I don't care! I just want to know that the place is tidy! I've got too much to do to worry about your room so will you just do as you're told for once in your life?"

"Whatever!" I pull the duvet up around my ears to block out the rest of her nagging.

14:00

"You've been quiet this lunchtime. Are you Okay?" Amber asks me as we leave the canteen and walk down the corridor towards the dreaded Room 13 – Double Physics – Yuk!

"Brian's coming back today," I say, expecting that to be explanation enough.

"So?" she replies.

"Oh never mind. It doesn't matter."

"Suit yourself!" she shrugs.

Steph would have understood. She always understood how I felt. I really miss Steph!

20:00

"Hi there, gorgeous!"

"Hi, you sexy hunk of beef!"

Brian and OB snog each others faces off in front of me. It's soooo embarrassing. I mean they seem to have completely forgotten I'm even here!

"Don't mind me!" I say as I walk away from them and go and sit in the living room. "Fetch me a bucket someone, please!"

20:05

"I thought someone must've superglued your faces together!" I say as they finally walk into the living room.

"Sorry, Kiddo. Your mum and me had some serious catching up to do," slimes Brian as he produces a gift-wrapped box from behind his back and hands it to me. "I got this for you when I was in Tunisia. I thought you'd like it."

I open the box to reveal a beautiful silver necklace. I've never seen one quite like it before. There are silver and coloured glass balls threaded onto the silver chain. My friends are going to be soooooo jealous!

"It's an authentic Berber necklace," Brian blushes slightly as he waits for a response.

"It's cool. Thanks," I reply.

"You can have your present later!" he winks at mum.

Saturday 8 December

I'm worried about OB since a police woman who came to our school yesterday to talk about domestic violence. She's been acting weird since Brian came back.

08:00

"Is there any more tea in that pot, Ron?" Brian asks as he drains his mug.

"That'll be stewed by now anyway. I'll make some fresh," OB replies and jumps up to make another pot.

"I should think so too! And be quick about it, Wench!" Brian slaps her on the behind as she walks past him. OB gives a little yelp and then giggles as she crosses the kitchen to fill the kettle.

Brian decides he's cold and goes to fetch a jumper from the bedroom so I seize the opportunity to talk to mum about my concerns.

"Mum?"

"Mmmm?"

"Are you happy with Brian?"

"Of course I am! Why do you ask?"

"You just seem...different when he's around."

"I'm just happy he's here, I suppose," she shrugs.

I knew it! She's covering up for him. True, they seem all smiles during the day but the walls between our rooms are thin and I can hear the shouting and noises at night. I'm sure he's hurting her. If she won't tell *me* what's going on, I'll have to talk to Elizabeth. She'll listen to her.

22:00

Oh no, it's started again! He's shouting at mum. It's been the same every night since he got back.

"Don't you tell me what to do, you bitch! While I'm around, *I* say what goes, do you hear me?"

"Yes, Brian."

Mum, it's your house – tell him where to go!

"What did you just call me?"

"Sorry, master!"

"That's better."

"No woman of mine tells me what to do. You'll have to be punished."

"Yes!"

"By the time I've finished with you, you're not going to be able to walk out of here! You'll never escape from me!"

I bury my head in the pillow to drown out the noises coming from her room. From the squeals and groans, it's obvious he's hurting her. If mum won't tell him to go, then I'm going to have to get us both out of here. As quietly as I can, I pack a bag with some clothes and other essentials and hide it under my bed so no-one will see it. I'll deal with mum's tomorrow.

Sunday 9 December

I have a plan. OB and I are getting away from here – today!

09:00

Great! OB and Brian have just nipped out to the shops. That'll give me time to pack a case for her. I run up to her room. That's funny? She hasn't made the bed. She's normally so strict about making the bed each morning as soon as she gets up.

Now, where's her suitcase? Ah, there it is! I can see it sticking out from under the valence frill. I cross the floor and pull the suitcase out from under the bed. This isn't the one she used for our holiday. Oh well, I haven't got time to look for that one. This will have to do. I unzip the case and open the lid.

"What on earth is all this?" The case is full of unfamiliar clothes. On top is a nurses uniform. That's weird? Mum's never been a nurse? Underneath is a maid's outfit, a police woman's uniform and some black PVC thing that looks like something the Cat Woman wears in the Batman films. I get it! It must be a fancy dress case. No wonder I've never seen it before!

09:15

Oh no! They're back! I've been so absorbed by the fancy dress case, I didn't realize the time! I quickly zip the case and push it back under the bed. I'll have to think of some other way to pack some things for her. I can hear someone coming up the stairs. What shall I do? I know! I run over to her cupboard and grab her hair straighteners.

09:16

"What are you doing in here?" OB asks as she walks into her bedroom.

169

"Sorry, my straighteners aren't working. I've just come to borrow yours. You don't mind do you?" I rush past her and head back to my room before she can answer.

20:00

It's worse than I thought! They were supposed to be going out tonight and he called her upstairs about half an hour ago. I thought they were going to get changed but I can hear the noises and banging going on in there. I don't think I've got time to pack a bag for mum. She could be in real danger.

20:01

I've made up my mind - I'm going to call the police. She might not thank me for interfering now but I'd rather have her cross with me than dead. I'll probably end up being given an award on the bravest person in the universe programme (or whatever it's called) next year.

20:02

"Hello? Yes, I'd like to speak to the Police please - It's my Mum. Her boyfriend's hurting her upstairs."

"Yes I can still hear them now."

"I can't see exactly what he's doing. The door's locked!"

"Yes, please send someone quickly."

I give the lady our address and telephone number and she promises to send someone round as soon as possible.

20:10

I'm almost hysterical by the time the police arrive. The noise has been going on for ages. My poor mum must be black and blue. I run to greet the policeman and woman as they get out of the car. They tell me to wait downstairs while they go and see what is happening.

20:11

They're coming back down! I can't bear to look!

"I'm so sorry to have bothered you Mrs Barrowman," the police-woman is smirking as she walks down the stairs.

"That's alright, you were only doing your job," I hear OB reply.

"Enjoy the rest of your evening, sir!" the policeman says as they walk out of the front door.

I hear mum close the door after them and can see them giggling as they get into their car.

"You stupid girl! I've never been so humiliated in all my life!" OB shouts from the door of the living room, before she runs back up stairs in floods of tears.

This is all too weird. I was only trying to help.

20:12

What *was* OB doing wearing that nurses uniform?

Monday 10 December

I seem to be in the doghouse today!

07:30

I walk into the kitchen. OB's very quiet as she pours hot water from the kettle into the tea pot. I catch a glimpse of her face as she fetches the milk from the fridge. She looks tired. Her hair isn't in its usual "fresh from the salon" state and her eyes are all red and puffy. She looks like she's been crying. I bet I was right after all. He has been hurting her!

"Are you alright, Mum?" I ask her. She might be a nagging old bag most of the time but she *is* my mum and I don't like seeing her upset.

"Just eat your toast and go to school, Anne," she replies.

She seems angry. Not only that - she seems angry at me! What have I done? It's him who's hurting her. I just tried to save her – ungrateful cow!

Brian walks into the kitchen. He's got a suitcase with him. Great! I didn't know he was going back already! OB looks round at him. She looks really sad. Why would she be sad about him going? You'd think she'd be relieved!

"Brian...please..." she looks really sad now. Her eyes are trying to say something to him, but I can't read what it is.

"I'm sorry, Ron. You're great...you're *really* great. I guess I'm just not used to having kids mess things up for me."

OB nods her head silently. Tears stream down her cheeks as she follows him to the front door. They hug for what seems like forever and then they talk some more. I can't hear what they are saying but there's a lot of nodding and shaking heads. He kisses her on the top of the head and walks away.

"Result! OB is finally safe from the wife (well, girlfriend) batterer!" I congratulate myself. I thump the table with the side of my clenched fist as elation rips through my body.

My head is filled with visions of the bravery award ceremony. Winner of the saving her Mum from domestic violence – even when the police were useless, category. I must work on my acceptance speech – or is it just the Oscars that have acceptance speeches?

My momentary high is brought crashing down to earth when I spot OB crumpled in a heap by the front door, sobbing uncontrollably. I'd better leave her alone for a while. I know what it's like when you break up with someone – even if they are unsuitable. She'll get over it quickly enough though – I did with Tom.

Thursday 13 December

Since Brian left, OB seems to have gone to pieces. She normally dresses smartly every day, regardless of what she's doing – but she's just thrown on her jeans and a jumper every day. AND she hasn't even bothered with make-up! This is not like her at all. She hasn't even nagged me for leaving my homework in the living room. – It's like she doesn't even care?

08:30

"Have you seen the notice board?" Amber runs over to me with Sarah and India as I walk through the school doors.

"Duh! I've just got here. How could I have seen it?"

They're obviously excited and are all squealing and jumping up and down as they all try to tell me the news.

"We're auditioning for the school show. Come and see!" Amber drags me by the arm to the school notice board.

There's a brightly coloured notice on the board asking for all budding actors, singers and dancers to audition for the school show, which is to be put on in February. Tom and Mr Hill (the music teacher) have written their own version of High School Musical and called it Our School Musical.

"How cool is that? I've already put our names down to audition. There's four main girls parts so I reckon we've got them in the bag." Amber brags.

"But we don't even know who else is auditioning!" I reply.

I look at the list of names beside the notice. It's only half past eight and already fifty people have signed up for auditions.

With only a week to prepare a song and a short acting piece, I don't share Amber's confidence.

"We can all practice round my house if you like," Sarah suggests. "We can use the conservatory. There'll be plenty of room to practice our dance moves in there."

Sarah and India instantly burst into a (it has to be said rather tuneless) rendition of Breaking Free from High School Musical.

"Distinctly average," I say in my best Simon Cowell voice.

"We'll be brilliant by the time the auditions are here!" laughs India.

"Whatever!" I reply

Saturday 15 December

Hooray! It's the last week at school this week.

08:30

I panic as I realize that I've left my Christmas shopping really late. I'm rubbish at remembering what presents I need to get. I always seem to forget somebody. Last year I forgot to buy anything for Belinda (or was that deliberate? I can't remember now!).

10:30

Armed with a list of who I need to buy for, I start to look around the shops. OB's easy so I pop into Boots to buy her favourite Jean Paul Gaultier perfume.

10:40

That was easy! I cross the main road and walk south towards my favourite shopping area – The Lanes. I'm sure to get some inspiration there. I love this collection of narrow passageways. It's full of the most amazing shops – not like anything you get in the main shopping area. The shops are all independent and you can find some really unusual gifts here.

During the summer there are normally buskers, portrait painters, masseurs, clairvoyants and the like dotted through the Lanes, but in the middle of winter it's too cold so the streets only have shoppers, probably all trying to find ideas for Christmas presents, like me.

I find the shop I've come here for. It's a really cool bohemian place that sells clothes and jewellery and all sorts of environmentally friendly gifts. Saffy, she used to go to my school until a couple of years ago, runs the shop with her mum.

I pick up a basket and wander around the shop, gazing at all the amazing things. I head to the jewellery section, where I immediately see a gorgeous ethnic necklace that I know Elizabeth will love. It's made with different coloured wooden beads and feathers and will look great with the boho clothes she wears. I pick out some cool bracelets for Amber, Sarah and India and head towards the clothes. I can't resist, when I see a really cute multicoloured hippie baby dress. Lilly will look like Mini-Me when Elizabeth carries her around with her in that!

I almost reach the counter when something really unusual catches my eye. On the shelf, are some psychadelic coloured doormats. How cool are they?! I walk over to take a closer look and the label tells me that they are made from recycled flip-flops. Brilliant! Nathan loves all that green stuff - and it'll look awsome in Elizabeth and his new flat. Feeling really pleased with myself, I take the basket to Saffy to pay for the gifts.

11:30

Along the narrow alleyway is a shop that sells ethically sourced gifts. I browse through the clothes. I find a matching scarf, hat and gloves for Dad, that are made from recycled jumpers. Ha! They've even got socks to match! It's always been a tradition to buy Dad socks at Christmas so I add them to the basket.

I find a really nice photo frame for Belinda. I'll put a picture of me in it. She'll have to put it on the mantlepiece so it'll be there to remind her how much she hates me! It's only small so I buy her a box of Fair-Trade chocolate brazils – such a shame she's allergic to nuts!

Along with some shiny red "responsibly sourced" (whatever that's supposed to mean?) wrapping paper, I head to the till to pay.

12:00

I normally buy for Mags, but she's not going to be here – and it doesn't look like I'm going to hear from Steph again so it's just the brats to buy for. I walk past the clock tower and head for the toy shop in Churchill Square.

I spend ages just looking at the huge display of toys on offer. In the end, I decide on a Bratz doll for Olivia (can't think where I got the inspiration for that one!) and a toy drum for Josh (he's going to drive Belinda mad!).

Sunday 16 December

Audition rehearsals round Sarah's. 10:00

08:00

I haven't even had time to think about what song I'm going to sing – never mind what short bit of script I'm going to use.

08:01

Don't actors always do Shakespeare for auditions? We've been studying Romeo and Juliet this term. I'll go and get my copy. There must be something I can use in there.

08:30

I decide on Juliet's "What's in a name?" speech. It's not too long so I think I can learn it by Thursday. I'll take it with me to Sarah's today and see what they think. Now, what song can I do? Everyone's bound to be doing something from High School Musical so I think I'm going to do something different. You know what they say – make sure you stand out!

08:31

Got it! OB took me to see "Fame" last year. There was a really nice song in that. I'm sure she bought the CD of the show because "it reminded her of her youth in the 1980s" – she must be really old if she was alive then! I'll see if it's on there.

12:30

We've been rehearsing for two and a half hours now – or to be more accurate, Sarah and India have. Two and a half hours of the same two songs from "High School Musical"! Amber and I haven't had chance to do anything yet. At this rate I think it'll take until Thursday before we get a turn.

"Sarah, this *is* supposed to be a rehearsal for all of us," moans Amber. "Don't you think Anne and me should have a go now?"

"Sorry, we got a bit carried away. What song are you doing, Amber?"

"When There Was Me and You." She grins. "You know, the one Gabriella sings."

I knew it! Another one from "High School Musical". I'm starting to worry that choosing something from another show might not have been such a good idea.

Amber starts to sing. I never knew she had such a nice voice. She doesn't sound like she needs much rehearsal to me. At least I won't have to worry about being given the main part. I don't think I want the romantic lead role. I'm more suited to the comedy support role – might as well keep it real!

"That wasn't bad," Sarah said as India and I applauded Amber's performance. "But don't be too disappointed when they make you my understudy."

"Well I think you'll get the part!" I blurt enthusiastically.

Sarah's glare made me realize that I'd made another gaff!

"So, what are *you* singing?" Sarah smirked as she looked at me.

"Erm..."Out Here On My Own"," I reply nervously.

Three blank faces stared at me.

"I don't remember that one?" India frowned.

"It was probably in "High School Musical - Two" – it was no-where near as good as the first one!" Sarah scoffed.

"Actually," I reply. "It's from "Fame.""

Thursday 20 December

I've become completely obsessed with the auditions. It's been all I can think about. The rest of the week at school has passed in a blur and every evening has been spent locked in my bedroom learning the song and speech.

16:30

I feel sick with nerves! The auditions started at eight o'clock this morning. There are so many of us want to audition, we've all been given a number and an audition time. The head gave permission, for those who needed to, to leave class to attend their slot. Lessons are over for today, which is just as well because I couldn't concentrate anyway!

They are running a little bit late so five of us are sat outside the music room, waiting for our turn. Now I know what it must feel like to audition for the X-Factor! I just hope they don't think I'm like one of the really bad ones that they make fun of. Mind you, from the horrible noise I can hear coming from the music room now, I don't think I'm going to the worst they've heard. I feel really sorry for her, whoever it is. Nerves have obviously got the better of her!

16:31

My jaw drops as I see who comes out of the music room.

"I was a bit nervous, but I think I managed to nail it!" Sarah smiled smugly at me as she walked away from her audition.

16:32

The five of us waiting for our auditions compare our allocated numbers. Bethany is next and then it's me!

16:35

As I listen to Bethany sing, I'm feeling even more nervous. She's pretty good. I hope I at least make a place in the chorus!

16:37

OMG. They've called my name. My legs have turned to jelly and I think the rest of my body's going the same way as I walk into the music room. There are three people sitting behind a desk (it really does feel like X-Factor!) but I'm too nervous to even notice who they are.

"So, what song from "High School Musical" are *you* going to sing for us, Anne?" I hear Tom say.

"Oh! I'm sorry. I didn't realize that the song had to be from that show." I reply.

I'm gutted. I've blown the audition before I even start!

"No, no! You don't have to. It's just that with everyone else choosing one I just assumed that you would be the same. So what song *have* you chosen for us?"

Tom smiles when I tell him the number I have decided to sing. I take a deep breath to steady my nerves and give it everything I've got. I look into Tom's kind eyes as I sing and lose myself in the emotion of the song. I can't believe how quickly it's over.

I've done it! I was so scared I'd mess it up. All I need to do is get through the monologue and then I'm out of here! Tom raises an eyebrow when I tell him the speech I have chosen. Is that a good thing?

Once again, I try to imagine that Tom is Romeo as I deliver my words. The minute that in rehearsals had seemed so long, flies by. I have no idea how it went as I leave the room – but I'm certainly relieved it's over.

186

Friday 21 December

I couldn't sleep last night. My audition kept buzzing through my head all night. I'm just thankful that we only have to wait until lunchtime, and not until next term, to find out who's in the show!

07:30

"You've seemed uptight this last few days. Is something wrong?" OB asks as she places a mug of tea in front of me.

"I'm fine," I lie.

She has no idea about the show. I don't like keeping things from her but this is my opportunity to make her proud of me, and I couldn't bear the humiliation of having to tell her I didn't even get into the chorus.

12:30

The atmosphere in the school assembly room is electric. There must be a hundred and fifty pupils in here and you could hear a pin drop, we're all so nervous. Tom walks out onto the stage with a sheet of paper in his hand. There is an audible gasp from all of us as he steps forward to address us.

"Thank you everyone for coming. First of all, I'd like to say what a delightful surprise the standard of the auditions gave us. This school has some very talented pupils, as I'm sure you are all about to find out. Thank you all for taking the time to audition. However, as you can see, there are simply too many of you to be able to give a part in the show to everyone, much as I would have loved to."

Just tell us who got the parts, Tom – PLEASE!

187

"Right, I'm about to announce the principal roles. Girls first."

We all hold our breath as he announces the four girl part. Bethany and Amber are allocated the two minor roles, which just leaves the bitch and the romantic lead. Sarah is looking very smug as she's confident that one of the roles will be hers. I'm just waiting for the chorus to be read out to see if I made it into the show.

"And playing the spoilt rich girl is Sophie Winterton!" announces Tom.

Talk about type casting! Stuck up Sophie squeals with delight as she is congratulated by her closest friends.

"And last but not least. An absolutely outstanding audition was given by one young lady. We had no difficulty in giving the main role to Anne Barrowman!"

"What?" Sarah gasps. "This can't be right!"

"Anne! That's fantastic!" Amber throws her arms around my neck.

I'm completely stunned! Nothing like this has ever happened to me before. OMG! What boy am I going to have to kiss? The next few minutes are an emotional rollercoaster – a mixture of fear and excitement as we wait for the boys to be announced. Toby and Gareth get the two minor roles. Who are the main ones going to be?

"And the brother of the spoilt rich girl is going to be played by Jack Bryson!" Tom announces.

Sarah is fuming as she realises that her boyfriend has got a major part in the show.

I can hardly bear to listen as Tom is about to announce the boy I'm supposed to fall in love with (and probably have to snog!) in the play.

"Another fantastic audition came from the person we have chosen to play the romantic lead male. I'm happy to say that the part goes to...Liam Grayson!"

Nooooooooo! Of all the boys in the school - they have to pick him! This is my worst nightmare! Liam blushes as he looks over at me. Don't you dare smile at me, Liam. Just because I have to act with you, doesn't mean I have to talk to you!

We wait as the names of the chorus are announced. India is delighted when her name is called out as the understudy for my part. Ten other names are called out and then...

"Well, that's our cast. I'm sorry to disappoint the rest of you. However, I can tell you that we *will* be needing help backstage so we would be grateful if any of you fancy assisting with the production. Well done everyone and we'll see you at the first rehearsal in January!"

"Idiots! They obviously don't know *real* talent when it's staring them in the face!" Sarah fumes as she storms out of the room.

17:00

"Anne, that's wonderful! I'm so proud of you." tears well up in OB's eyes as I tell her the news.

"I can't believe they actually chose me." I grin. "There *is* one problem though – they chose Liam to play opposite me!"

"Oh, I see," OB puts her hand to her mouth to try and hide her smile.

"It's not funny, Mum. I hate him! AND I've got to see him at the school party tonight!" I sulk.

"Of course you do," she nods. "Well, I'm sure that professional actresses get cast opposite people they don't like. You'll just have to show what a wonderful actress you are."

I hate it when she does that! I have a crisis and she comes out with some sensible advice. She always manages to make my disasters seem like nothing!

19:00

School's Christmas Party – the official end to the Winter term. After the excitement of winning the lead role in the school musical, it's amazing how much of a loser I feel right now as I walk into the party alone. I can see Amber, India and Sarah across the room and head towards them.

19:01

Oh Great! Gareth, Jack and Toby have just joined them – and they've got Liam with them! Well, well, looks like I'm not the only loser Liam! Where's your date for the night? I feel a little bit better about the situation as I reach my friends.
Sarah's face still looks as though she's been sucking lemons all evening. She's obviously still angry at not getting a part in the show. You'd think she could be pleased for the rest of us. I'd have been pleased for her if she'd got a part and I hadn't.

"Are you sure you're not too important to speak to us now you've got the starring role?" Sarah asks spitefully as I join them.

"Butt out, Sarah, she did really well!" Liam snaps.

"I'm sorry? I don't recall asking you to defend me. We mooses (at least I hope that's the plural of moose) have surprisingly thick skins - so I can fight my own battles thank you very much, Liam Grayson!" I reply.

I feel really pleased as all three of the guilty boys squirm with embarrassment.

"I was just trying to help," he mumbles.

"There you are, Liam! I've been looking for you everywhere. I thought you'd abandoned me," Sophie simpers as she curls her arms around Liam's neck and kisses him.

He's here with stuck up Sophie? Thanks a lot, Liam. My humiliation is now complete.

Monday 24 December

Christmas Eve! I hope OB's remembered that we're not doing the pillow case thing this year.

17:00

OB and me are just finishing off the Christmas tree decorations as a familiar voice call out.

"Hi, Mum!"

Elizabeth and Nathan have arrived with Lilly. They're staying here tonight because Mum wanted to see every minute of Lilly's first Christmas.

"Hello, darling. Is my little grand-daughter looking forward to her first Christmas?" OB asks her as she kisses to top of Lilly's head.

"I don't know about her, but we're really excited! We've come prepared." Elizabeth grins as she holds up three empty pillow cases that she has brought with her.

Honestly she's so childish!

19:00

I carefully place the presents that I've bought for my family under the tree and stand back to admire it in its full glory. I have to admit, OB and I have done a good job. The decorations and presents look spectacular!

"It looks lovely doesn't it," smiles Elizabeth as she appears by my side. "I love Christmas! It's going to so special this year with Lilly."

"You're right. It *is* going to be special this year!" I reply as she puts her arm around my shoulder.

"We'd better get to Dad's. I promised him we'd drop their presents off for them this evening," she sighs.

"Okay," I nod as I pick up the carrier bag that I have left their presents in.

19:30

Dad and Belinda had already cracked open a bottle of champagne and both have half-empty (or is it half-full – I never know which?) glass in their hands as Elizabeth and I arrived. He offers Elizabeth a glass.

"I'd better not," she replies. "I'm driving - and we can't stay long as I've got to get this one to bed. She's getting a bit over excited!"

"Elizabeth is of course talking about Lilly and not me!" I point out.

"Oh, so you won't be wanting any presents tomorrow then?" Dad teases me.

"Duh! Of course I do!"

He leads us into the living room and we place our presents under their tree (which I'm pleased to see is not as nice as ours!). Elizabeth puts theirs under the tree first and then it's my turn.

"Five presents?" Dad raises an eyebrow at me. "Are they all for here – there's only four of us?"

"I bought two for Belinda this year as I forgot her last year," I smile sweetly.

194

"Oh that's very sweet of you. She'll be touched."

Not when she sees them I smile to myself!

Tuesday 25 December

Hooray! It's Christmas!

07:00

I'm woken up by sounds of OB and Elizabeth giving Lilly her breakfast. I jump out of bed and race to the door of my bedroom to collect my usual pillowcase full of presents.

07:01

What's going on? There are three bulging pillow cases outside Elizabeth's room but nothing outside mine.

07:02

"Where's my pillowcase?" I ask miserably as I walk into the kitchen.

"Your present's under the tree – remember? It's what you said you wanted," OB replies.

Damn! I'd forgotten about that!

"I was just testing. Pillowcases are for kids anyway!"

I flounce out of the kitchen and head back up to my bedroom to get dressed, feeling a bit jealous of the fun the others will have discovering what delights their pillow cases hold.

07:15

As I emerge, fully dressed, from my bedroom, I meet Nathan on the landing. He looks disturbingly like Russell Brand as he yawns and tries to smooth down his bed-hair.

197

Begrudgingly, I help him carry their sacks of goodies down stairs.

We all gather round to start opening presents. OB hands me an expertly wrapped parcel. I guess that it's the MP4 that I have been wanting, which is excellent. I carefully unwrap the package, taking as long as I can as it is the only one I'm going to be opening from Mum this year.

"Thanks, Mum. It's exactly the model I wanted," I smile, trying to hide the fact I'm disappointed not to have a sack of presents.

OB smiles back at me as she curls her arm around the back of her chair.

"I thought you might like this to go with it," she grins as she drags out a large pillowcase full of presents.

"Nice one, Mum!" I say as I run over to her and throw my arms around her.

Maybe I'm not quite ready to grow up just yet!

15:00

After a hectic morning of opening presents and helping Lilly try out all her new toys, we had Christmas dinner. As usual, OB had gone completely over the top and had prepared enough food to feed us three times over. OB did manage to spoil it a bit when she kept complaining about how little I was eating. She finally shut up when I told her that I was just leaving some room for the cold supper we will have later (another of our family traditions which consists of the leftovers being brought out of the fridge to be eaten with a selection of pickles - after we've sat around the table playing cards or games).

OB's now busy re-loading the dishwasher. Lilly and Elizabeth are fast asleep on the sofa and Nathan is reading Peter Kay's autobiography (a Christmas present from OB). I decide to go and have some quiet time in my room and listen to my new Arctic Monkeys CD.

15:30

OB knocks on my bedroom door and puts her head around the door.

"I've got someone here to see you," she smiles.

"Can I come in?" a familiar voice asks. "I couldn't let Christmas go by with us not speaking!"

"Steph!" I gasp. "Come in!"

Steph walks into my room with a huge grin on her face and carrying a box covered in magenta foil wrapping paper. The smile disappears as she sees me.

"Bloody Hell!" she exclaims. "What've you done to yourself? You look like a stick insect!"

"I've just been on a diet. You haven't seen me for a while, that's all!" I smile.

"I'm sorry. Diets are supposed to make you look better. I hate to say it but you look bloody awful. You can't weigh more than six stone!"

"Don't exaggerate! I haven't lost that much!" I laugh.

"Have you looked at yourself in the mirror lately?" she asks.

"I've given up with scales and mirrors," I reply.

199

"Well you can start again, right now!" she says crossly. She grabs my arm and drags me to the bathroom to the scales.

"Go on – get on!" she demands.

For some reason, the sheer determination in her eyes makes me do as she tells me. I step onto the scales. Rather than look at the readout, I look at Steph, whose face has turned from fear to horror.

"Anne! Get a grip of yourself. You weigh six stone two!"

"What? But that's impossible! I've hardly lost any weight at all!" I shake my head in disbelief.

"Look at yourself, Anne! You're practically wasting away!"

I can't see it - but I have to believe her. Steph, of all the people I know, would never lie to me. I'm confused. How could this have happened? I only wanted to lose the excess weight I was carrying. Could OB have been right all along?

"I didn't realize!" I said to Steph and, for no reason at all I burst into tears.

"It's Okay," she said kindly. "I'm here. I'll look after you."

"What am I going to do?" I ask her.

"It's easy – you're going to start eating again. And you can start with these!" she said as she handed me the box she had brought in with her.

"I didn't buy anything for you." I admitted, feeling ashamed as I opened the wrapping. I could tell by the shape of the box that it was a box of my favourite chocolates.

"Oh well, looks like we'll have to share these then doesn't it!" she giggles.

"Cheek!" I laugh as she helps herself to one of the chocolates.

"Well, what else are friends for if not for sharing!" she grins. "Go on – get one down you!"

"It's good to have you back, Steph!" I smile as I pop a chocolate into my mouth.

CHAPTER SIX
Love, Relationships and Weddings

Monday 7 January

It's so good to have Steph around again. It's been tough, but she's been helping me put some weight back on. I've laughed more in the couple of weeks with her since Christmas than I have in the past few months put together.

07:00

Steph made me make a New Year's Resolution to put weight *on*! She has appointed herself as weight monitor. She insists that I weigh myself every day and give her an update over the phone as to how my weight is going. It's like being in a Weight Watcher's class – but in reverse!

"Six stone six!" I proudly tell her.

"Excellent! Four pounds in two weeks. Award yourself a Mars Bar after lunch!"

"Er...I'm a bit off Mars Bars at the moment!" I reply.

"Really? Well any other chocolate bar then! And don't forget your three "Celebrations" after dinner!"

"I can't put *all* my weight back on with chocolate!" I laugh.

16:30

Amber, India and me walk to the Assembly Hall. I'm both nervous and excited as today is the first rehearsal for the school show. We are among the stragglers as we wander into the room. Tom is standing up on the stage, waiting for the last of us to arrive.

"Come on, ladies. Hurry up!" he cries. "We've got a lot to get on with today.

He does a quick head count and seems satisfied that the whole cast is here. Someone closes the door as he claps his hands to gain our attention.

"So as everyone is involved in the initial rehearsals we have decided to work on the group scenes and musical numbers first. Principals will have extra rehearsals to practice their own scenes. I expect 100% effort and commitment to this show if it is going to be ready in time for February. Are you all still up for this?"

"Yes, Tom" we reply.

"I SAID ARE YOU ALL UP FOR THIS?"

"YES, TOM!"

"That's better!" he smiles. On the front of the stage is a copy of the script for everyone. Come and collect a copy and then take a seat. We're going to work on two numbers that involve the entire cast today. You will probably all be familiar with the songs so it shouldn't take too long to get those sorted. Miss Brown, who some of you girls will already know as our dance teacher, has agreed to do the choreography for the show. Once we've got the music sorted, we will clear the chairs and I'll hand you over to her!"

17:00

This rehearsing is more difficult than I thought it would be. We've only just got used to the lyrics when it's time to pack up the chairs and learn the dance routines. Now this should be fun!

18:30

"La La La, La La La La La," I sing to myself as OB drives me home.

"Not too many lyrics to learn in that one then!" she laughs.

I'm too shattered to bother with a response!

Thursday 10 January

All that singing and dancing seems to have renewed my appetite. I can't seem to stop eating. I'm feeling fitter and stronger already!

07:30

"Six stone seven!" I announce to Steph.

"Are you sure? I'll be checking at the weekend," she replies.

"You're worse than my mum! I'm thinking of changing your name to MB!" I tell her.

"What's that stand for?"

"Mini Bag!" I laugh.

17:00

I'm really nervous! Liam and me have got a big love scene to practice. It's based on Romeo and Juliet. Tom has also set the class a project for our English study of Romeo and Juliet and he wants us all to act out and film a scene from the play. Liam suggested that we film the rehearsal as our part of the project. Like an idiot, I said Okay, before I remembered that I'm not actually talking to him!

My hands are shaking as I press the doorbell to his house. I just hope that we can get through this without arguing!

"Hi!" he smiles as he opens the door.

"Hi!"

"Er...Come in."

"Thanks."

Well if we're going to be this awkward with each other on stage this show is going to be hideous!

Liam shows me through to the living room, where he has set the video camera up.

"We can rehearse each bit and then film it when we're ready," he suggests.

"Okay," I nod. "This is going to be soooo embarrassing!"

18:00

The rehearsal is going really well and we've got most of the scene filmed. I gulp as I look at the script and notice that the next bit is THE KISS!

"I think we should just go for this bit. There's only a few words to say and we can get it out of the way then!" he blushes.

We both check our lines and switch the camera back on.

"It's no use, our friends will never accept us being together," I attempt to sound distraught.

"I don't care what the other's say, we're meant to be together. As soon as I saw your face I knew you were the one," we both try not to giggle as he repeats the lines from the script.

He moves in towards me and my heart skips a beat as he kisses me. This kiss doesn't feel like it's part of any script, it feels real to me! We sink onto the sofa and forget all about the camera as we continue to snog.

18:10

"The camera! I panic as I realize it's still recording. "It's been filming us kissing!"

"It's Okay. I'll erase that bit," he blushes as he grabs the camera and flicks a switch to erase the last part of the film.

"What about the rest of the scene?" I ask, remembering all the work we had put into the bit before the kiss took over.

"I've only rewound a bit, the rest should be fine," he promises.

I leave his house completely embarrassed. Though I must admit, the kiss was pretty good!

Saturday 12 January

Belinda's revenge!

11:00

The moment I've been dreading is finally here. I sit on Dad's sofa waiting for Belinda to come downstairs with the bridesmaid's dress she has chosen for me. Her friend, Cassandra, is sat waiting with me. She's a wedding dress designer and has come to make the final alterations to Belinda's dress.

"I'm so excited I found this, Anne. The colour is going to look wonderful on you," Belinda says as she carries the dress downstairs.

I don't know what she's chosen yet, but it's bound to be horrendous. She'll have picked out something really embarrassing for me to wear all day - just to humiliate me

"Well, what do you think?" she beamed as she held up the monstrosity in front of her.

It's a satin copper meringue with huge puff sleeves and gigantic frills around the neck and the shirt is covered with layers of bronze and cream sheer organza. Even worse, it's massive! I'm no expert, but it looks like a size 20 or something!

"It's...big," I say.

I knew those Christmas presents weren't a good idea. She's got the perfect opportunity to take her revenge out on me now! To my surprise, she bursts out laughing.

"No, you silly girl!" she snorts. "I mean the colour. It's gorgeous isn't it. I bought a big one so Cassandra can work her magic on it – you just wait and see!"

"I think I can do something with that," Cassandra nods as she gets her tape measure out.

"Make sure you don't make it too tight," I warn her. "I'm trying to put weight on."

"Well, that's a first!" she smiles.

15:30

Cassandra is amazing! She has completely re-made the dress. It's now got a strappy top and a straight skirt that ends just below my knees. She's made the organza into a wrap and a matching headpiece.

"I think Cassie can finish the dress without you now, Anne." Belinda smiles happily. "Now it's time to finish *my* dress."

Great! I can't wait to see what Cassie has made for Belinda. I bet it's really awesome.

"Your mum will be here in a minute, Anne."

"Oh, but I wanted to stay and see your dress!"

"I'm sorry but no-one is going to see the dress before the big day – except Cassandra and me."

Humph! And to think I was almost getting to like her!

Sunday 13 January

Hooray! It's snowing!

08:00

I watch through the kitchen window as the snow falls and marvel at how beautiful it looks as it settles on the trees and the rooftops. We don't get snow that lays that often but it's falling fast so I'm feeling quite hopeful.

10:00

There's a knock at the front door. I open the door to see Steph standing on the doorstep – or at least I think it's her. I can just about see her face, which is looking extremely pink, under her big coat, woollen hat and scarf.

"Wooooh!" she woops. "Get your coat on…it's snowball time!"

I laugh as Steph starts to run about our front garden doing some sort of crazy snow dance. As I look out at her, I can see that there's about two inches of snow on the ground. More than enough to make snowballs with! Excitedly, I run upstairs to get my thick sweater and coat. I emerge in my battle gear of boots, jeans, big coat, woolly hat and even bigger scarf. I'm not letting Steph get me in the face with a snowball.

10:30

I can hardly feel the cold as we run around throwing freezing lumps of snow at each other. It continues to snow so the supply replenishes itself quickly enough. I howl with laughter as I dodge a missile that Steph had aimed at me and it hits OB in the face (who had come out to see if we want some hot chocolate)

Tears stream down my face as Steph trips and falls face first into the snow. Typical of Steph, she just laughs it off and turns over on the ground to make a "snow angel".

11:00

We go inside the house to take up OB's offer of hot chocolate. It's only when the house feels so hot that I realize how cold it was outside. Steph has me laughing so much as she tells jokes while we drink our chocolate that I almost wet myself and have to beg her to shut up!

I'm so glad that Steph's my best friend again. No-one makes me laugh like she does. This morning's been so much fun and there's no way I would have had snowball fights with Amber and Sarah.

Tuesday 15 January

Today was the most embarrassing day of my life!

07:30

"How much?"

"Six stone thirteen!" I repeat, feeling rather proud of myself for getting up to a respectable weight so quickly.

"Well done! I'm proud of you. You're gonna look great in your dress on Saturday." Steph congratulates me.

"Thanks." I reply and we say goodbye.

08:30

I walk to school feeling really good about myself. Steph has been such a fantastic friend. I'm so grateful that she made me see sense before things got too out of hand. My "eating my way back to health" regime has worked brilliantly and I feel happier and stronger than I have in a long time.

11:00

English! It's Liam and my turn to have our Romeo and Juliet project shown. I cringe as Tom puts the tape into the machine and hide head in my hands so I don't have to watch.

"It's no use, our friends will never accept us being together," I hear my voice say.

Hold on a minute, that's not the beginning of the scene? My head jolts up and I stare at the screen.

"I don't care what the other's say, we're meant to be together. As soon as I saw your face I knew you were the one," Liam says and I pray that the tape will stop.

The entire class wolf whistle as they watch Liam kiss me on the screen. Why isn't the tape stopping? Liam was supposed to have deleted this bit. I feel my face burning as I watch us getting stuck in on screen. The class are in uproar and start cheering and banging the desks. I can't breathe!

"Ahem - Well that's one way to do Romeo and Juliet, I suppose," says a red-faced Tom as he turns off the tape.

Totally mortified AGAIN, I run from the class.

"I'm sorry," I hear Liam call behind me. "I must've deleted the wrong bit!"

I run as fast as my feet can carry me to the girls' room. Tears of humiliation are streaming down my cheeks. I run some cold water to rinse my face as Amber enters the room.

"Tom sent me to see if you're okay," she smiled.

"I can't believe he's done it to me again!" I sob.

"Liam made a mistake. He thought he'd deleted the end of the tape but deleted the beginning instead."

"Really?"

"Mind you, that was one hot kiss!" she giggled. "Are you sure you were just acting?"

As if I'd be interested in an idiot like that!

Friday 18 January

I have decided that I'm going to ignore childish boys making kissing sounds every time I pass them today. I am going to maintain my poise and dignity at all times!

09:00

"Hey, Anne. Gissa snog!"

"Mwa Mwa Mwa!"

"Oh Romeo, Romeo – Take me! Take Me!"

These boys aren't even in my class. The whole school must know about it by now! I remember my promise to myself and smile sweetly at them.

"Maybe when your penis is as big as your mouth, you might stand a chance!"

OMG I can't believe I actually just said that! Still, it seems to have had the desired effect as their friends roll about laughing as I walk off with as much dignity as I can manage.

04:30

"Hey, Anne!"

Oh no, here we go again!

"Wait for me!" Liam calls as he runs to catch me up. "I'm really sorry about what happened. I honestly thought I'd deleted the kiss bit."

"Amber told me," I reply coolly.

"Do you think you can forgive me?" he asks with a cheeky grin.

"I s'pose so," I shrug.

"We'd better get to rehearsal then."

"Yeah, Tom'll be wondering where we are."

"I heard what you said to James and the others this morning. They were well gutted! Hilarious!"

"Yup, that's me! Comic genius!"

We laugh again as he puts his arm through mine and walks me to rehearsal. Well if we're going to have to act together, I suppose it's better if we can be friends.

Saturday 19 January

Yes! Seven Stones exactly. Am extremely pleased with myself as I've reached my target weight for the wedding!

08:00

"R U NERVOUS?" a text message from Steph asks.

"A BIT" I reply.

"UL B GR8 – CUL8R"

"OK"

I'm relieved that Steph is going to be there at the wedding. I'm not going to know many other people, other than Dad and Belinda – and they'll be too busy to be bothered with me today!

08:10

As I walk into the living room, I can see that OB's been crying. She wipes her eyes with a tissue and smiles sadly at me.

"Are you sure you're Okay with me being a bridesmaid today?" I ask.

"Of course!" she tries to smile again. "It's just that it all seems so final today somehow. I know the divorce was final - but knowing that he's marrying someone else today..."

I give her a hug as she starts to cry again. I don't understand adults at all. If she still loves my dad – how come she divorced him?

10:00

OB drops me off at Dad's house and drives away before she can get upset again. Dad's not here. He spent the night at a hotel so that Belinda could have the place to herself to get ready for the wedding.

Belinda's best friends, Cassandra, Sabrina and Melody, are both here. Cassandra is busy checking the dresses as Melody finishes Belinda's hair. Sabrina makes a start on her make-up as Melody grabs me to sort my hair out.

11:00

Belinda, Olivia and I stand together for a photograph as we wait for the car to arrive. Olivia looks cute today. Cassandra made her a dress out of the excess material from the one she made for me. She's got a simple copper coloured top and she has made a ballerina skirt out of the rest of the organza to match my wrap.

I have to admit that Belinda looks stunning in her dress. The ivory satin gown looks beautiful against her complexion. She looks radiant as she sips champagne with her friends. She *does* seem really happy to be marrying my dad.

11:05

A white Rolls-Royce turns up to take us to the wedding. A grey-uniformed chauffeur gets out of the car and calmly walks up the path to ring the doorbell. Belinda's friends leave for the Registry Office. Belinda and me check that we (and Olivia) are all ready, pick up our bouquets and head out to the waiting car.

11:15

We arrive outside the Town Hall, where the Registry Office is. Belinda looks nervous as we walk up the steps past the four huge white pillars into the reception area. We walk up the massive wooden staircase to the ceremony room. Dad is already waiting with my Uncle Jonathon (who is his best man), Josh, who looks surprisingly sweet in his little suit, and the other guests. His face lights up when he sees Belinda.

While we wait to be called into the ceremony room, I stand with Olivia and watch the people going about their business below us from the ornate balcony. Elizabeth, Nathan and Lilly have promised to keep Steph company until I can free myself to be with her. They wave at me from the other side of the waiting area as the Registrar calls us in.

15:00

After the ceremony, the wedding party moved to the reception, which is at the golf club that Dad is a member of. We arrived and had to endure endless photographs being taken in the grounds outside. I'm so glad that bit is over as I hate having my photo taken. Once that was over, I was at least able to join Elizabeth and Steph for the dinner. However, we had been "volunteered" to look after Josh and Olivia. For once, they were fairly quiet and kept Lilly amused while we ate.

The tables were cleared away to reveal a dance floor and a band starts to play. Dad leads Belinda out onto the dance floor. I can't remember a time when he looked happier. Soon everyone else is up dancing and the party is in full swing.

"These are a lot better than you normally hear at weddings." Steph shouts over the music as they start to sing a version of OutKast's Hey Ya!

Typical of Steph, she starts to sing along loudly and jig around uncontrollably to the music. She really doesn't care what she looks like as long as she's having a good time!

"Anne! I've someone here that I'd like you to meet." I hear Belinda say as she approaches me.

I turn round to see that she has a nervous, although quite dishy, boy of around my age standing next to her.

"This is Jeremy," she says. "He's my cousin. I though you and Steph might like to keep him company as there's not many of your age around here."

"Sure, why not," I shrug.

Jeremy blushes at he sits next to me. I needn't have worried about him being shy though because Steph soon has us both laughing with her antics and she never shuts up long enough for him to have to talk much anyway!

19:00

"Would you like to dance?" Jeremy asks me as the band start to play a smoochy number.

"Okay," I reply.

I feel pretty nervous as we walk onto the dance floor. I've never danced with a boy before. I hope I don't tread on his toes or something equally as embarrassing.

"I'm glad I got you up here. Your friend's hardly shut up all afternoon," he laughs as we sway to the music.

"Oh Steph's not so bad when you get to know her." I smile.

"I'm sure she's great – but it's you I want to get to know." He replies.

I can't believe it! Somebody actually fancies me!

20:00

"We'd better get back to Steph," I giggle as yet another song ends. "We've been up here for ages!"

Tonight is the best night ever. Steph is on good form and Jeremy has hardly taken his eyes off me since we came off the dance floor. He's really cute. I wonder if I'll see him again after today?

23:00

The wedding party all cheer dad and Belinda off as they leave to go on their honeymoon - somewhere in the Maldives, I think but I'm not sure exactly where. Elizabeth and Nathan are staying at Dad's house to look after The Brats while they are away. Lilly's tired so they decide to take the children home.

"How are you getting home?" Elizabeth asks me as she hands a sleeping Lilly to Nathan.

"I'm going to ring Mum," I reply. "She said she'd come and get us."

"Okay, well don't leave it too late."

"I won't," I promise as she kisses me goodbye.

I phone OB to come and fetch us and then Jeremy whisks me onto the dance floor for a final smooch.

"I've really enjoyed today," he says as he puts his arms around my waist to dance.

"Me too," I admit.

Please ask me out! Please ask me out! I pray as we move together in time to the slow beat. The song ends and he takes me by the hand and leads me back to the table where Steph is sat watching us.

"I'd like to see you again...I mean, if you'd like to," he stammers.

"That'd be great, " I reply as I grab my bag for a pen and paper (OB was right all along, it does come in handy!) "Here's my mobile number...and here's my telephone number...oh and here's my e-mail address!" I frantically scribble the details onto the piece of paper and hand it to him.

"Right, thanks," he laughs. "I'd better go - Mum and Dad are gesturing that they want to leave."

"Okay," I grin. "See you soon then!"

"I'll call you," he mouths as he walks away.

"I wasn't too desperate was I?" I ask Steph, who is staring at me open mouthed.

Monday 21 January

Yes! Jeremy phoned last night. We're meeting for a coffee after I've finished rehearsal tonight.

07:30

"So, where's this *Jeremy* taking you?" OB asks.

"We're going to Lorenzo's for a coffee."

"Okay. I'll pick you up outside there at seven-thirty."

"No way! He'll think I'm a baby!"

"It's a school night - and you'll still be needing your dinner," she raised her hand in a "don't even think about arguing" sort of way.

"But, Mum – that's sooooo embarrassing!" I whine.

"I want to see what this boy is like so it's either that – or you're not going at all!" she replies.

She's got that look on her face (she's looking at me over the top of her reading glasses and her lips are set in a stern straight line) I know I have got no option than to back down or I'll risk being grounded or something. As a token mark of protest, I pick up my bag and stomp out of the kitchen.

"It's soooo unfair!" I hear OB mock as I open the front door to leave for school.

22:00

I can't sleep! I'm so excited after tonight.

The rehearsal went really well and the show is starting to come together brilliantly. I was already in a good mood when Jeremy met me from the school gate. I made sure that I left the rehearsal with all my friends so that they could see I'VE GOT A BOYFRIEND!

Lorenzo's was fairly quiet so Jeremy and me could talk and get to know a bit more about each other. He's fifteen and is on the school rugby team. He wants to be a solicitor when he leaves school. He's always been secretly envious of Belinda and he thinks my Dad's really cool. (At least that saves me the embarrassment of introducing my new boyfriend to my Dad!).

We got on really well and the hour we had together flew past. I was completely gutted when it was time for OB to pick me up. I think he likes me because he's asked to see me again on Saturday – and he kissed me on the cheek before I got into the car.

22:30

Still thinking about Jeremy – sigh. Think I have finally found *the* one! I'd better practice my married signature.

Anne Dowling

Mrs Anne Dowling

Mrs A …

OMG! Have just had a horrible thought! Jeremy is Belinda's cousin. Belinda is now married to my dad. Does that count as incest?

Saturday 26 January

Have had the best week ever! Jeremy has sent about 50 text messages a day and my friends are all sooooo jealous that I've got an older boyfriend!

I have been feeling particularly pleased with myself this week at school. On Wednesday, after seeing me with Jeremy, all my friends came up to me and said the same thing.

"Who was that (hunk/hottie/cutie) I saw you with last night?"

"You mean Jeremy? Oh he's my boyfriend!" I'd reply (acting really casual)

They're all jealous – and they were even greener when I told them he's nearly sixteen! I feel soooo sophisticated now I've got an older man!

19:00

Jeremy and me are attempting to set Steph up with his best mate Jason. We arranged to meet at the cinema and "bump into" each other. It doesn't seem to be going too well at the moment. We went for a drink before the film and I couldn't believe it when Steph didn't say a word – I mean Motormouth never shuts up normally! Lets hope that things take a turn for the better at the cinema.

17:30

Jeremy and Jason return from the kiosk with arms full of popcorn and coke. We show our tickets to the usher and go and find a seat in the back row! We get settled in our seats and pass the cartons of coke and boxes of popcorn along the line so that all of us have got some. I snuggle up to Jeremy and he puts his arm around my shoulder as the opening credits start.

Jason sees that Jeremy has his arm around me and tries to do the same to Steph. Suddenly she lets out a deafening shriek and jumps out of her chair, sending her coke and popcorn flying all over the rest of us. She runs out of the cinema so we decide to leave the film and go to look for her. We can't find her anywhere. I check the toilets and even ask the lady at the kiosk if she's seen her. She's disappeared. I try to text Steph to see where she is, but there's no reply. Jeremy sends Jason home and walks me home.

On our way home, I receive a text from Steph.

"2 MBRSD 2 C NE1 – AM ON BUS HM"

Poor Steph must have sneaked out of the cinema and headed straight for the bus home. I think I'll let Steph find her own boyfriends in future!

CHAPTER SEVEN
So How Many Did You Get?

Friday 1 February

With less than a week to go, the school show has practically taken over my life. Jeremy and I don't have a sex life, we have a text life!

16:30

"Have you heard the latest about Abi?" Amber asks me as we walk into the rehearsal room.

"No, what's happened?" I reply.

"She's had the baby this afternoon!"

"You're joking! It's not due until next month."

"I just got a text from her. She's had a little girl – Mia," Amber tells me excitedly.

"India and me are going to see her after rehearsals. Do you want to come?"

"Definitely!"

She picked a bad place to tell me the news because Gareth overhears our conversation. He steps into our path and blocks us from walking any further into the room.

"Did you just say Abi's had the baby?" Gareth looks visibly shocked.

"What's it to you?" Amber snorts.

"It's *my* kid!" he replies "I've got a right to know!"

I know he's treated Abi badly, but I feel sorry for him. He's got a point. It *is* his baby.

"If you really want to know, she's in the hospital," I tell him. "We're going to see her later if you want us to give her a message."

"No thanks. I'm coming with you," he replies.

Tom claps his hands to get our attention for the start of the rehearsal. Amber glares at me as we go to take our places for the singing.

18:30

We arrive at the hospital and find the private room that Abi's mum and dad have paid for. Abi's asleep as we walk into the room so we decide to take a peek at the baby while we wait for her to wake.

"She's soooo tiny" Amber whispers.

"She's adorable," India agrees.

Gareth steps forward nervously to take a look at his daughter. His eyes fill with tears as he looks at the tiny little bundle. I actually think he's going to cry.

"She's amazing," he croaks as Mia sleeps peacefully.

"What's *he* doing here?" Abi's voice breaks the silence.

Our presence must have woken her. Gareth steps away from Mia's cot and moves towards Abi's bed.

"I had to see her," he said quietly.

I have visions of him walking across to her bed and sweeping her up in his arms. Pictures fill my mind of us all throwing confetti at their wedding and grinning inanely, like in some Sandra Bullock Rom Com.

"Go to hell, Gareth!" Abi cries as she turns over onto her side with her back to him.

Obviously Abi didn't read the script!

Saturday 2 February

Have had boyfriend for two weeks now.   Am practically engaged!

11:00

February is not the most romantic time to be walking along Brighton seafront. It's freezing cold but I don't want Jeremy to think I'm not enjoying myself so I pull my scarf up around my face a little bit more and take hold of his hand.

This is now our third actual date, although it feels like we have been together much longer than that. I suppose it could be something to do with the long text conversations we have every day. The cold wind makes me shiver and Jeremy pulls me towards him. He puts his arms around me and holds me close to him to protect me from the cold. As I look into his eyes, he looks down at me and smiles. At last! He's going to kiss me!

He does. It's a soft, gentle kiss. Okay, so I didn't feel fireworks go off, like I did with Liam, but it was nice anyway. That's Jeremy through and through really – nice.

11:15

We arrive at the pier. The good thing about having a boyfriend who's got money is that he can afford to pay for us to try out any of the rides we dare to go on.

"First one to wimp out on a ride, pays for lunch!" he laughs as he holds up a handful of tokens.

We warm up by having a go on the Carousel and the dodgems. Then we go into the penny arcade and Jeremy buys me some candy floss.

"Right, down to business. First we are going into the Horror Hotel. Are you up for it?" he smiles wickedly.

"Okay, but we go in separately," I reply.

"Why?"

"Because I don't want to be with you when you cry like a baby!" I laugh as I run towards the ride.

From the outside, it looks like most other fairground ghost trains. Except it's bigger and the new trains are nice. We get into the train and it moves off. As we enter the enclosed spiral hill lift, Jeremy pulls my woolly hat down to over my head, which makes me squeal.

"Told you, you'd be scared!" he laughs as I push my hat off my face.

"That's cheating!" I reply as we enter the main area of the ride.

It was a fun ride though, sort of like some cheesy old black and white horror film, rather than proper scary. I climb out of the train feeling confident that I can match him for bravery on any ride. Then we reach the Super Booster. I'm much more nervous as we are strapped into this floorless ride. There is only a small bike saddle to sit on and my feet are dangling in the wind. I begin to regret agreeing to go on the ride as we are winched slowly to 100 feet with nothing but the sea below us. I shut my eyes and wait for the drop. I probably look like something out of Wallace and Gromit with my mouth drawn back behind my ears as we drop almost to the floor. The giant arm then swings us back and forwards over the sea and the pier. It's really exciting.
Jeremy looks green as we are let off the ride so we find somewhere to sit for a while.

"Okay, you win!" he grins as the colour returns to his cheeks. "Lunch is on me!"

Sunday 3 February

Good news! Jeremy texted me to say that Jason happens to like eccentric girls so he wants to meet Steph again – will see if I can persuade her when I see her later!

12:00

I have spent the whole of the morning practicing for the show in my bedroom. There's so many lines to learn! Everyone else seems to remember theirs at rehearsals but I keep forgetting mine – and we've only got another week until the show opens!

Some of the cast have even started to make fun of me (which isn't fair because I've got more lines to learn than anyone else – except maybe Liam and stuck up Sophie!)

Talking of Sophie, I heard that Liam and her have broken up. I don't know what he sees in her anyway. She doesn't even have to act when she's being bitchy to me in the show. Gareth and Jack apparently told Amber that he was only going out with her to make me jealous anyway. NEWSFLASH LIAM – IT DIDN'T WORK!!

14:00

Missie jumps up onto the bed in Steph's bedroom. She gives a loud purr and rubs her blue-grey body round us as we try to talk. That cat is so nosey, she can't stand to be left out of a conversation and tramples all over you until you stop ignoring her and fuss her.

Once she is satisfied that she is still centre of attention, she yawns and settles down in between us, curling her tail around her so it covers her eyes to enable her to sleep. I finish telling Steph about my day with Jeremy. Suddenly Steph sits forward and lets out a huge sigh. She pulls her legs up in front of her and rests her chin on her knees.

"You're soooo lucky having a boyfriend like Jeremy – he really likes you – and he's cute!" she sighs again.

"You could have a boyfriend if you wanted one," I reply.

"Boys are never interested in me. Even when they are, I just end up making an idiot of myself – I mean look at the other day at the Cinema – I looked like a complete dork!"

"That must be why Jason wants to see you again then!" I grin.

"Really? He's not some sort of head case is he?"

"Probably!" I laugh. "Jeremy thought you both might like to come ten-pin bowling with us next weekend."

"I can't believe it! I'm going on my first date!" Steph flings herself backwards onto the bed in excitement.

I can see I'm going to have to teach her how to be more grown up if she's going to have an older boyfriend like me!

Thursday 7 February

Am devastated. Jeremy has only sent me ten text messages today – I think he must be going off me!

Saturday 9 February

OB has decided to hideously embarrass me by inviting just about everyone we know to see the show!

11:00

"The college has accepted me on the Childcare Course, Mum," Elizabeth smiles. "Thanks for lending me the money to enrol. I couldn't have done it without you. Nathan's going to look after Lilly one night a week while I attend the classes."

Huh! She never lends *me* any money – not even when I really needed that new top to go to Steph's mum's fortieth birthday party last year!

"That's fantastic news darling!" OB says as she throws her arms around Elizabeth. "I'm so proud of you!"

Oh right, so she gets pregnant and drops out of Uni. Mum has to pay for her to go back to college – and yet she's proud of *her*! I scowl as I watch them both making a fuss of Lilly, who's sat in her pushchair blowing bubbles from her mouth. OB is kneeling by the pushchair and she looks up at me, as if she is expecting me to join in their lovely little scene. A frown creases her forehead as she sees my scowl.

"What's the matter with *you*?" she asks.

"Oh nothing!" I reply sarcastically. "I've got better grades at school so far than either Elizabeth or Mags got AND I've got the lead part in the school show – but you never say you're proud of me. Why should anything be wrong?"

"Of course I'm proud of you!" OB looks taken aback. "Why else would I have invited all our friends and family to come and see you in the show?"

243

"You've done what?" I gasp as she stands up and walks towards me.

"I was so excited that I've told them all to come," she smiles as she reels off a list of people that she has cajoled into coming to see me, grandparents, aunts uncles, cousins, neighbours – even the old lady that I used to walk the dog for when I was ten (until the stupid thing got loose from it's lead and ran out into the road, straight in front of the Number 2A bus!).

"How could you do that to me?" I howl. "That is just going to be sooooo embarrassing!"

"I just can't win with you can I?" she says, throwing her arms up in the air dramatically.

Duh! You could always try not being such an idiot, Mum!

Sunday 10 February

Double date - Ten-Pin Bowling with Steph, Jeremy and Jason today. At least it should keep my mind off the big opening night tomorrow!

11:00

We arrive at the bowling alley. There's a counter where we have to go and pay for the game and get kitted out with the bowling shoes. That's the only bit I'm not so keen on. The idea of wearing shoes that have been on hundreds of other people's feet doesn't exactly thrill me.

We walk along to the end of the huge line of bowling lanes. It's already busy with friends and families all here for a giggle. The atmosphere is buzzing as everyone seems to be having fun.

"First game – Boys against Girls!" Steph announces as she sets up the machine. "Me and Anne are going to thrash you!"

"We'll see about that!" Jason laughs as he finishes tying his shoes up.

In the first round, (sorry, *frame* as Jeremy keeps correcting me!) the boys both did well, Jeremy scoring two strikes and Jason managing to knock seven pins down and getting the other three with his second ball. Steph amazed me by getting two strikes. My first ball left my hand and rolled into the gutter along side the lane.

"Here, let me show you!" Jeremy sprang to my rescue. He took hold of my bowling arm and guided the next ball down the lane for me."

"Wooooh! Eight!" I cry in delight at my achievement.

245

Jeremy and Jason sat down, looking extremely smug with themselves as if they knew they had the game in the bag if I was going to be this rubbish!

"What the hell are you playing at?" hissed Steph. "You're good at bowls normally!"

"Steph, don't you know anything about playing a game with boys. You have to let them win or they'll be in a strop for the rest of the day. I'm pretending to be rubbish but will get better as the game goes on. That way, when they narrowly beat us, Jeremy will think he taught me how to play so well!"

"I don't get it – why should we have to lose just to please their overblown egos?"

"Trust me, Steph!" I smile knowingly. "If you want Jason to like you - don't beat him!"

Honestly, Steph just doesn't understand men at all!

11:30

I continued with my plan for a few games and the boys seem to be enjoying showing their skills off to us. Knowing that they are beating us fairly convincingly at this point, their chests visibly puff out before they take their turn to roll the ball down the lane.

"Watch this," Steph whispers to me as her turn came round.

She's determined to get another strike and picks up her ball and places her fingers in the little holes. She takes an extra long run up to the lane. Her face is a mask of concentration as she holds the ball up in front of her and lets it swing back past her hip in a perfect bowling action. Her arm swings forward and she trips on the lace of her shoe, which has worked its way loose. She stumbles almost half way down the lane and tries to release the ball. Her finger is stuck and the ball speeds along the lane – with Stephanie still attached to it.

"Nooooooooooo!" she cries as she slides head first into the pins.

The gate of the machine closes behind her and we are all helpless with laughter as all we can see are her legs sticking out of the machine that collects the pins. When he manages to pull himself together, Jason runs to find someone to help get her out of the mechanism.

13:30

They have finally managed to release Steph from the machine at the end of the lane. I don't think the men who came to fix it were too impressed with her! As they walk away, Steph turns to me with a big smile on her face.

"At least I still got a strike!"

It would have been nice to have been able to finish the game but the manager didn't see the funny side of it and came over to tell us that we were no longer welcome in the bowling hall! Some people just don't have a sense of humour. My only regret is that I didn't have a camera on me – it would have made a classic for "You've Been Framed!"

Monday 11 February

My plan of using our feminine guise seems to have worked. Steph texted me to let me know that Jason has asked her out on Saturday!

19:00

I've been so nervous all day at school that I was hardly able to concentrate on our lessons. I thought that was bad enough but I feel physically sick as I stand at the side of the stage, waiting for the curtain to rise.

Tom and the backstage crew have done a fantastic job with the stage. It looks amazing! The opening scene has a backdrop of colourful graffiti on a wall and some scaffolding that we get to climb on during the dance numbers. It looks really cool!

I smile to myself as I remember the good luck text that Jeremy sent me while I was still in the dressing room. He's so sweet!

I can hear the audience coughing and shuffling in their seats as they wait for the school band to start to play. Mum and Elizabeth are out there somewhere. I just hope I can't see them because I'm sure I'll mess up if I can see OB blubbering or something.

Liam winks at me from the other side of the stage and I feel my stomach flutter. It must be the nerves. I tell myself. Suddenly the band start to play the first few bars of the opening number and the curtain opens, revealing a sea of expectant (and rather nervous) faces in the audience. Oh no! OB and Elizabeth are in the front row! I gulp as I count the bars for my entrance. Oh well, here it goes!

20:30

That was absolutely amazing! We've got through the show without a hitch. I have never felt such a buzz in my life. I feel totally exhilarated as I walk back to my dressing room (one of the cubicles in the girls PE changing room).

20:40

The cast all sound like a bunch of real luvvies as we all congratulate each other after the show.

"You were fantastic!"

"Oh no, I was rubbish - *You* were fantastic!" etc...

Actually, I think we were *all* fantastic!

We hang our costumes in the lockers, which have been hijacked for the next week, and make our way out to the school entrance hall. There are lots of squeals and kisses as friends and families greet the performers that they came to support. I spot OB and Elizabeth at the back of the entrance hall and push my way through the crowd to meet them. As she sees me, a big grin breaks out on Elizabeth's face. OB's eyes are all red - she's obviously been crying. For the first time in my life, I can see real pride on her face as she holds out her arms to me and I run into them.

"I'm so proud of you," she says as she kisses me on the cheeks and hugs me.

"You were brilliant!" Elizabeth smiles.

"Really?" I'm amazed by their reaction.

"You were awesome, Titch!" says a familiar voice.

There's only one person who still calls me Titch - and she's supposed to be thousands of miles away. I hardly recognise the suntanned woman with sun-bleached blonde hair. What happened to her curly mop of red hair?

"Mags? I didn't know you were going to be here!" I squeal with excitement.

"Yup, I came all the way from Israel just to see you!" she grins.

"Actually, I got a postcard from her last week," OB admits. "I thought it'd be a nice surprise for you to see her today."

"It's brilliant!" I laugh.

22:00

Laying in bed, I'm still on a high. The show was fab – and Mags being home is sooo cool! For a first night, I think we did really well. The audience seemed to love the show and Liam and me got the biggest ovation at the end. I would soooo love to do this for a living.

22:30

I definitely want to be rich and famous when I leave school. Maybe I should go on X Factor and win it. Then I wouldn't have to get some boring old office job which hardly pays your rent. Either that or marry some rich footballer, then I could just have loads of money and not have to do anything other than pose and look pretty.

22:31

Actually, I think it would be pretty boring being a WAG. I'm far too independent to want to live off somebody else's fame! Will have to win X Factor or Britain's Got Talent or something instead.

Tuesday 12 February

Today, I had a glimpse of what being famous must be like!

12:30

From the moment I got to school this morning, I realized that the show has caused a commotion. So many people have come up to me to congratulate me, or to wish me luck for tonight, that I've lost count. It's weird really. Even people who never spoke to me before are talking to me! Suddenly, I feel like I really *am* somebody. You'd think we were the cast of the *real* High School Musical, the way they've all been acting!

17:00

"Mum, I'm too nervous to eat!" I protest as OB puts a plate of poached eggs on toast in front of me.

"You need to keep your strength up, Titch, if you're going to be able to get through those dance routines tonight." Mags says before OB has a chance to speak.

"I s'pose so." I reply. Mags has an infuriating habit of always being right!

"Thank you," OB mouths to Mags. She thinks I didn't see her – but I did!

20:30

"I don't care what the other's say, we're meant to be together. As soon as I saw your face I knew you were the one," Liam speaks the last line of the show.

My heart races as he steps forward to kiss me. I know it's only part of the show but tonight feels different. My knees

253

feel weak and the kiss seems to last forever. Maybe it's just that he's more used to kissing me now, but it feels much more real than it did last night! I'm sure I see him blush as we pull away from each other to sing the last song.

20:40

Dad, Belinda and Steph are waiting to greet me as I walk out into the entrance hall.

"Hi, my little superstar!" Dad greets me with a huge bear hug. He squeezes me so tightly that I can hardly breathe.

"Thanks for coming Belinda," I smile sweetly at her as she stands next to my Dad.

"I wouldn't have missed it for the world," she replies.

Yeah, you probably hoped I'd fall flat on my face!

"Wow! How brilliant were you?" Steph gushes as she throws her arms around me.

"Thanks!"

"Who's the one who nearly snogged your face off at the end? He's gorgeous!" she asks.

"Oh, Liam? He's Okay, I suppose," I reply, hoping that Steph can't see me blushing.

"Jeremy *will* be jealous when he comes to see you tomorrow!" she winks.

"He's got no reason to be," I tell her. "As if I'd fancy *Liam*!"

"Yeah, right!" she shakes her head. "More like, who wouldn't?"

"NEWSFLASH!" I shout. "I'VE GOT A BOYFRIEND!"

Thursday 14 February

Valentines Day! I hate this day. Every year it's the same, I get one card – from my Dad!

07:30

I walk into the kitchen and OB is busy making scrambled eggs on toast for Mags and me. On the table lay three coloured envelopes. One is addressed to Mum, and has already been opened.

"Who's your card from, Mum?" I ask casually.

"It's from Brian!" she replies.

"Brian! What does he want – sending you a card?" My bottom jaw drops so far it almost hits the table as I speak.

"I don't know," she sniffs. "It's in the bin!"

"Good!" I say as I lift the other two cards off the table.

The first envelope is bright yellow and I instantly recognise the handwriting that has addressed the envelope to me. Every year at school there seems to be a competition to see who got the most valentines cards. Always the same question – How many did you get? A couple of years ago (when I was just a kid) I was so upset that I had to yet again answer the question with "none" that Dad sent me a card. He's sent one for the last couple of years, to save me the embarrassment of having to admit to having no cards.

I smile as I open the envelope and look at the front of the card, which shows a sweet little grey boy kitten in a blue jacket saying I love you to a white girl kitten with a pink bow in her hair. It's really cute.

Inside my Dad has even written a poem.

Roses are red
Violets are blue
Here's a card to remind you
Your Dad still loves you!

"That is soooo naff, Dad," I laugh as I pass it for OB to see.

A pink envelope is also addressed to me. Yes! I've got my first real valentines card! I tear the envelope open as quickly as I can manage and a warm feeling washes over me as I see the card.

To My Girlfriend on Valentines Day

The front of the card shows a picture of a cartoon couple in a lovey-dovey pose in the middle of a big heart. The boy is giving the girl some flowers. I've never had anyone buy *me* flowers – maybe Jeremy will buy some for me this year?

Inside, the card simply reads

Can't wait to see you after the show tonight!

Jeremy
xx

I should have known he wouldn't let me down!

Mags walks into the kitchen, yawning and wiping the sleep from her eyes. She's holding a red envelope in her hand. Maybe she met someone in Israel, I think to myself – or maybe JB is trying to get back with her?

"This was on the doormat," she says at she chucks the envelope onto the table in front of me.

"For me?" I ask. I'm totally gob smacked.

"Well, you were still called Anne last time I spoke to you!" she rolls her eyes at me.

I can't believe it! For years I've never had a valentine card and now I get two! I bet it's from Steph, mucking about or something. I open the envelope and, on the front of the card is a simple red rose. Something about it tells me that it's not a joke. Nervously I look inside the card. There are no shop printed words, just a hand written poem.

There's a missing space within my life
that only you can fill.
For I have loved you from the start
and I swear I always will.

I'll come to your dressing room after the show tonight. We need to talk!

L

Xx

My mind is in turmoil. What am I supposed to do? OB has always brought me up to know that you can't have two boyfriends at once.

"What's the matter?" OB asks as she sees the frown on my face.

I tell her who has sent the two cards and how I feel about both boys. Do I choose Jeremy? Sweet, kind, dependable, gorgeous Jeremy. Or do I choose the boy who makes my heart leap? I can't even explain to her why he does that.

"I think that some things are best left to fate," she says wisely.

"What do you mean?" I ask.

"Well, both boys are going to see you tonight after the show. Why not ask fate to send the boy you should be with to you first?"

"Do you think that could work?"

"It's worth a try," Mags nods. "Anyway, if the wrong one turns up first, you can always go for the other one instead!"

20:40

"Anne!" Amber calls as she knocks on my dressing room door. "There's someone to see you.

Which one will it be? Has Liam got changed quickly and got to me first, or has Jeremy come straight here from the audience. My heart is in my mouth as I open the cubicle door.

As I step outside into the changing room, all doubt is erased from my mind. I left the decision of which one to choose up to fate and, as I see the love on his face, I know that fate made the right choice. He's the one!

THE END

OTHER BOOKS BY THIS AUTHOR

THE MAGPIES

Magpie – *(Latin Pica Pica)* a striking bird of the corvid family, renowned for it's attraction to shiny objects.

Angel and Tommy Wilde are attracted to the bright lights and glittering life style that fame has to offer – but a shared dream of fame is where their similarities end. She is the daughter of classical musicians. His childhood was dominated by domestic abuse.

Tortured by his past, Tommy battles with drug addiction. Angel is desperate to save him and gives up her own dream of success to help him. The story chronicles the struggle of the aspiring rock band as jealousy, discrimination and drugs enter their lives with tragic consequences. Could the love they share be enough to save him or will their differences tear them apart?....

Lightning Source UK Ltd.
Milton Keynes UK
17 May 2010

154288UK00002B/432/P